THE LAST B

ATHACHA APPANAH, a French-Mauritian of Indian origin, as brought up in Mauritius and worked there as a journalist efore moving to France in 1998. *The Last Brother* was awarded the 2007 FNAC Prize for Fiction, and was also hortlisted for the Femina Prize and the Medicis Prize.

OFFREY STRACHAN is the award-winning translator of ndreï Makine.

"It half-reveals an extraordinary episode from the Second World Var, but through a lyrical mist that never clears away. In Geoffrey Strachan's sumptuous translation, we follow a fairy-tale flight from rsecutions, small and large, that bonds two boys from different ds of a suffering earth."
BOYD TONKIN, *Independent*

"*The Last Brother*, beautifully translated by Geoffrey Strachan, is d with the economy and sensuous detail for which the French *nte* is known. The rich implications of history and the complex olitical and social hierarchies that lie behind its comparatively mple story would have won the admiration of Marguerite urcenar."
PAUL BINDING, *Times Literary Supplement*

ppanah has created a notable study of guilt and redemption rough love, pure and absolute. Geoffrey Strachan's translation ears witness to a powerfully lyrical and poetic piece of literature . . . that staggers in its power to move the most cynical reader."
DOMINIC O'SULLIVAN, *Irish Examiner*

There aren't many publishers' lists about which I can say this, but I've never read a MacLehose Press book that I thought less than brilliant. And *The Last Brother* is no exception."
DANIEL HAHN, *Bookseller*

Nathacha Appanah

THE LAST BROTHER

Translated from the French by
Geoffrey Strachan

MACLEHOSE PRESS
QUERCUS · LONDON

First published in Great Britain in 2010 by MacLehose Press
This paperback edition first published in 2011 by

MacLehose Press
an imprint of Quercus
21 Bloomsbury Square
London, WC1A 2NS

First published as *Le dernier frère* by Editions de l'Olivier, Paris

This book is supported by the French Ministry of Foreign Affairs, as part of the Burgess programme run by the Cultural Department of the French Embassy in London.

A CIP catalogue reference for this book is available from the British Library

ISBN 978 1 84916 401 6

10 9 8 7 6 5 4 3 2 1

Typeset in Galliard by Libanus Press, Marlborough
Printed and bound in Great Britain by Clays Ltd, St Ives plc

TRANSLATOR'S ACKNOWLEDGEMENTS

I am indebted to a number of people, including the author, for their advice and assistance in the preparation of this translation. My thanks are due in particular to Nathacha Appanah, Christopher MacLehose, Damian Nussbaum, June Elks, Pierre Sciama, Simon Strachan, Susan Strachan and Wendy Wilson.

I

I SAW DAVID AGAIN YESTERDAY. I WAS LYING IN bed, my mind a blank, my body light, there was just a faint pressure between my eyes. I do not know why I turned my head towards the door, since David had not made a sound, not a sound, not like the old days when he used to walk and run a bit lopsidedly and I was always amazed that his thin body, with those legs and arms as long and slender as the reeds that grow beside streams, his face lost amid the soft hair that floated like spindrift from waves, I was amazed that all of this, this combination of small, gentle and inoffensive things, should make such a clatter on the ground as David walked along.

David was leaning against the door frame. He was

tall, and this surprised me. He was wearing one of those linen shirts whose softness and lightness excites envy, even at a distance. He had adopted a nonchalant pose, his legs slightly crossed, his hands in his pockets. A kind of glow bathed one side of his hair and his curls gleamed. I sensed that he was happy to see me after all these years. He smiled at me.

It may have been at this moment that I realized I was dreaming. I do not know where it comes from, this sudden awareness, I wonder why the real world sometimes invades a dream. On this occasion I found the vague sensation most unwelcome and struggled to convince myself that David really was there, simply and patiently waiting for me to wake up. Alright, I told myself, I'm going to tease him, say something to him like you're showing off, you're striking a pose, but I could not utter a sound. I made a superhuman effort, opened my jaws wide, trying and trying, but in vain, my throat dried up, it is incredible how real this felt, great gulps of air streaming in through my open mouth and parching everything inside. At that moment I sensed that I was on the brink of waking but I thought if I lay still the dream would last. So I stayed in bed, I closed my mouth, I went on looking towards the door, but I could not quell the sadness which had arisen in my heart.

At the very moment when this grief swept over

me, David came closer. With one supple movement he slipped his shoulder away from the door frame, his hands still in his pockets, and took three steps. I counted. Three steps. David was tall, strong, adult, handsome, so handsome. Then I really knew I was dreaming and could do nothing about it. The last time I had seen him he was ten years old. And yet here was my David in front of me. An incredible tenderness radiated from him, something indefinable which I had been aware of at precious moments in my life: when I lived in the north as a little boy and had my two brothers; and when I spent those few summer days with him in 1945.

Lying there in bed like that I felt a little ashamed. I was no figure in a dream. I had had sixty long years since that time with David and, flat on my back in bed, I could feel every day of them. Over all that period I had never dreamed about him. Even at first, when I used to think about him every day, missing him so much that I wept and wanted to die, he had never appeared to me in a dream. If only he had come earlier, when I was rather more like him, young and strong. I, too, could stand like that once, head held high, hands in pockets, back straight. I, too, could show off, strike a pose.

By stretching my neck, and raising myself a little on my elbows, I could have made out his face more clearly, but I was afraid to move. I wanted the dream to last, to go on, I wanted David to draw near of his own accord. Two steps more, I reckoned, and he would be close enough to touch and see. I should finally be able to look him in the eye. I could spring up, give him a friendly jab, hug him, doing it all quickly before I woke, somehow contriving to take the dream by surprise. Would he still have that broken front tooth, the one he had scraped against the ground as I dropped him, when we were playing at aeroplanes? I used to hold him flat out, his hands in front of him. He laughed and shouted as I hurtled forwards for several yards. He was so light. But I stumbled. Down on the ground, David went on laughing and I was the first to notice his broken smile, his lips all bloody, though he kept on laughing. He loved playing at aeroplanes, he wanted to do it again, he had no time for crying over himself. Otherwise, with all he had lived through up to the age of ten, I think he would have been weeping from dawn till dusk.

They say you have strange dreams when you are close to death. For a long time my mother used to dream my father appeared to her, dressed in his brown uniform, ready to go to work. Come with me, he would say, I need you. In her dream my mother refused point-blank, she told me, with a trace of alarm in her voice, she who had never refused him anything much during his lifetime. The night my mother died in her sleep, could it be that she had finally had enough of saying no and followed my father into the darkness?

But David, for his part, said nothing to me, he remained there, patiently watching me, between shadow and light. The dust motes hovering there in the first rays reminded me strangely of sequins. In the end it was pleasant, a dream at once sad and delicious, there was a lilac-coloured glow in the room and I told myself he could easily have carried me now. I have become a frail old man and if we were to play at aeroplanes again and he accidentally let go of me, as I had let go of him more than sixty years before, my whole body would be broken.

Suddenly I had had enough of waiting, I reached out my hand to him and it was morning, my room empty, the light dazzling, David vanished, the dream gone, my arm outstretched, outside the bedclothes, numb with cold, and my face bathed in tears.

* * *

I rang my son not long after having my breakfast. I asked him if he could drive me to Saint-Martin, he said of course, whenever you like, I'll come at noon today. My son is his own boss, he has little time for anything apart from work, he is unmarried, has no children, rarely goes out, hardly rests at all. But for the past few years now he seems to have had all the time in the world for me. It is because I am old, the only family he has left, and he is afraid.

At twelve o'clock sharp my son was there. I had been ready for a good hour before. When you grow old you are early for everything, you are fearful of missing things, and then you get fed up with waiting for people. I put on dark trousers, a blue shirt and a light jacket. As in the old days, I slipped a little beige fine-tooth comb and a carefully folded white handkerchief into the inside pocket of my jacket. I also took out the little red box and kept it in my hand. I thought with a smile that I looked rather like a man about to make a proposal of marriage. I should have liked to polish my shoes but the mere thought of such an operation exhausts me. So I sat down and rubbed both sides of my shoes against the living-room carpet as best I could, which made a sound that lulled me a little. When I heard the purr of the engine at the gate I stood up, waiting for my boy and leaning on my stick, as if standing to attention.

It is a new car, all grey and shiny. Metallic grey, my son specifies proudly. He makes no comment on my clothes, helps me into the car, fastens the seat-belt for me, adjusting it so that it is not too tight, puts my stick on the back seat and every time our eyes meet he gives me a big smile that draws his cheeks towards his ears and makes creases around his eyes.

He talks about his work briefly, he is in information technology, but it is difficult to talk about computers to an old man like me who understands absolutely nothing about them. So then he talks about his staff, young people he trains, who leave him very quickly, because, my son says, that's how it is for people who work in computers, it's changing all the time. When I tell him we are going to the Saint-Martin cemetery he says, that's fine, *papa*. No problem. It is probably no surprise to him that I should go to the cemetery. Most of my friends are dead now, we are folk who have had tough, hard-working lives and inevitably we die early, worn out and, if anything, eager to get it all over with.

My son puts on some classical music, checks that the windows are fully closed, adjusts the temperature in the car to twenty degrees, keeps within the speed limit and every time he brakes a little abruptly he reaches out an arm to protect me. I should like to tell him not to be so afraid for me, afraid for himself.

At Saint-Martin we drive down a road of earth and sand where great acacia trees have shed thousands of tiny husks. The car is jolting now and this wakes me up. I have known for many years that David is in this cemetery, along with those others who died from exhaustion, dysentery, malaria, typhus, grief, madness. During the early years, when the memory of David never left me for a moment, I was too young to come here and face this. Later on, I would set myself dates for coming here – my birthday, the anniversary of his death, the New Year, Christmas, but I never came. It looks as if I lacked the courage to do so and, if the truth be told, I thought I should never manage it. And now, today, because I had dreamed about David, it seems to me easy, obvious, I am not afraid, I am not sad.

The cemetery is very well maintained. It is surrounded by a low wall of red brick of the type used for the English houses. The graves topped by the Star of David are lined up in rows of ten, facing the electric-blue sea, metallic-blue, my son might say. With the trees all around them, these stars look as if they were waiting for the sky to come down to them. When David told me the star he wore round his neck had the same name as him, I was sure, at the age of nine, that he was pulling my leg. I was furious. Do you take me for an idiot, I retorted, raising my voice. But then what did I know about the Jews and the Star of David?

My son helps me to get out, hands me my stick and I walk forward, on my own. I locate David's grave on the plan at the entrance. My son is back in the car, I know he is watching me but all the same I take the comb out of my pocket and tidy my thick, grey mane of hair, which has neither thinned nor become limp with age. I straighten up, fasten the first two buttons of my jacket, pull down my shirt-cuffs and proceed. David is over to the east, he must be one of the first to be reached by the sun in the morning. I walk slowly, trying to make the anticipation last, as I had in the night, when I tried to make my dream last. I am reading the names on the graves, images jostle one another in my head, memories come back so strongly that I am aware of their weight on my chest, I see their colours in my eyes, feel the taste of them in my mouth and I have to slow down, inhale deeply and swallow to calm them.

And suddenly, brutally, it takes my breath away. After sixty years, I thought I was ready, I thought I should be able to confront this. Oh, David! I so much wish I was mistaken! I so much wish it could have been different. I wish I had never had to see this.

David Stein

1935–1945

The grave is just like the others and with sadness I picture his little-child's body and his blond hair within this great tomb. He is forever ten years old. And there it is again, I am the one who has survived and I am at pains to know why. I have led a plain life, I have done nothing remarkable . . .

I kneel down, my bones crack, my body is riven with shooting pains and my awareness of my own inner frailty is almost a source of pleasure. At last, *at last*, it will be my turn soon. I wipe the dust and sand from the black granite with my handkerchief. When it is clean, well and truly gleaming, I place the little red box upon it which contains his Star of David. And now I do what I did in my dream: I reach out my hand to David, close my eyes and remember.

2

UP TO THE AGE OF EIGHT I LIVED IN THE north of the country, in the village of Mapou. It was not a village such as exists there now, with clean houses, roofs in brilliant colours, roads of well-packed earth or asphalt, lined with elegantly trimmed bamboo hedges, painted wooden gates, opening into welcoming courtyards, flowers, vegetable plots, fruit trees, light and the play of shadows everywhere. When I think of it now, and I have no difficulty in recalling those years, the place where we lived seemed more like a rubbish-dump.

Starting at the edge of the vast cane fields, an undulating mass of green on the Mapou sugar plantation, there was a straggling line of boxes, huts, so-called houses, fashioned from whatever our elders could lay their hands on, and this was known as "the camp". Branches, logs, bits of wood, tree stumps, leaves of sugar cane, twigs, bamboos, straw, dried cowpats, they were endlessly inventive. I do not know how I survived life in the camp, how the frail and timid little boy that I was managed to survive those eight long years. In those parts as soon as a child fell ill, the family at once prepared its funeral pyre and as a general rule they were right to do so, illness led routinely, inexorably to death.

The camp stood on land where nothing grew, since enormous rocks lay beneath the surface and occasionally, during the night, swelling like plants, they would break through the reddish soil a little way. Just enough for people getting up before dawn or children running about wildly to bang their feet against them. Then the one injured would alert the others and a bamboo or a tree branch tipped with a scrap of cloth would serve as a warning. That is how I remember our camp, dotted about with warning stakes, which we had to put up with, weaving and winding our paths and our lives around them.

On days when the sun shone, which is to say for nine months of the year, an acrid red dust arose from the soil and it dogged us all. And woe betide us if the wind got up, for then, like a bullet from a gun, the mountain on the far side would send us a howling blast laden with this grit that came swirling around our wretched dwellings and seemed bent on only one thing: burying us once and for all.

But it was a mistake to pray for rain. Even at those moments of fury, when the dust entered every one of our pores, coalescing in crusts around our mouths and eyes, cramming itself into fine lines beneath our fingernails, even when in the morning we were spitting out brownish bile and our meals ended up tasting of this dry, acrid detritus, it was a mistake to pray for rain. For here, at Mapou, the glistening rain which falls from heaven, fine and gentle, almost like a caress, the rain which refreshes and for which one thanks heaven, such a manna did not exist. At Mapou the rain was a monster. We could see it gathering strength, hugging the mountain like an army rallying before an assault, hear the orders for battle and slaughter being given. The clouds would daily grow larger, so heavy and greedy that the wind which, down below on the ground, was making us stagger could no longer drive them away. We would raise our eyes towards the mountain, while the dust granted us a respite, and the sighs of our elders would prepare us for the worst.

The earth, which you might have supposed to be thirsty after so many days of sunshine, battered by the wind, pummelled from inside by burning rocks, this earth did not save us all the same. When the first drops of rain came pelting down on the camp it soaked them up for a brief while and became soft and light. You could plunge your foot into it, I remember that warm sensation around my toes, and we had visions of a fertile land, of vegetables flowing with sap, of fruit bursting with juice. But this did not last long. Even we, the children, who delighted in that first glorious downpour, our faces washed clean of the red dust, even we abandoned our games to take refuge in our homes. The earth was very quickly sated and the raindrops bounced off it like thousands of jumping fleas, with an intolerable rattling sound. This was the signal the largest clouds were waiting for. They exploded with a blinding flash, the thunder shook the earth and we ended up pining for the dry days and the red dust.

Within a short while a mudslide, laden with dead rats caught out by the rain up above in the cane fields, swept through the camp. Some of the huts began to shake and their occupants yelled out in fear, seeking refuge with their neighbours. In our house, that is to say in the single room that served us as a house, we sat there, dejected, watching the inevitable oozing of drips from the ceiling, praying that the walls would hold. We could hear cracking, creaking, thunderclaps, drumming, shouts. We did not stir, with knees pressed up against our chests, heads sunk into our shoulders, we waited and prayed. When at last silence returned, with the sun shining so intensely it seemed to be oblivious of the deluge, we had to begin all over again. Rebuild, clean everything, seek out and, inevitably, in the case of the most unfortunate, mourn those lost.

In the middle of the cane fields stood the Mapou sugar factory and several times a year its chimney belched forth thick steam which swirled above us slowly and luxuriantly. I loved its voluptuous white clouds with their rounded edges, as if drawn by a loving hand, and for a long time I wished I could spend the rest of my life inside them. I believed one could be very happy there curled up within them and leaping about among their coils. All the men in the camp, including my father, went to work in the cane fields. My mother, for her part, worked with various other women in the homes of the "bosses", as they were called. These bosses were the owners and managers at the factory. My father went off very early and my mother would leave our hut two hours later. My mother came home at the end of the afternoon and as for my father, well, he came home when he came home, always drunk, shaking and incoherent, flinging his arms and legs about like a disjointed marionette.

I had a brother one year older than myself, whom I loved more than anything in the world and a little brother a year younger than myself who, I believe, loved me more than anything in the world. Anil and Vinod. And me, Raj.

I remember how I constantly tagged along after Anil and how Vinod, in his turn, tagged along after me. In the camp as soon as a child was able to walk or more or less understood what you were saying to it, it ceased to be a child, it had a role to play, tasks to perform. My first memory is very clear in my mind. I do not know what Anil had done or failed to do, but my father is holding his head in the crook of his arm, and with the other he is lashing my brother's buttocks with a very green bamboo cane, all ribs and knots, with a very fine tip. My mother stands weeping at the door, her hands over her ears, and suddenly, beside me, Vinod hurls himself at my father, attempting to snatch the cane from him and my father, with a thrust of his elbow, flings my little brother to the other side of the room and my mother rushes over. From where I am I cannot see Anil's face but I remember my father having him at his mercy and the only weeping I can hear is first that of my mother and then of Vinod, but he, my big brother, does not weep.

Later, when I was an adult, when my father was dead, and my son already in his teens I told my mother that story. She doubted whether that memory could be my own, I was too little, she said, barely four years old. She thought I must have heard it from Anil, but I know it is my first memory of the camp at Mapou. That scene where I remain a spectator and where it is my younger brother, aged three, who comes to Anil's defence, while I am the one who should have done that. *Me*. When I think again about that first memory of my life it also seems as if I was keeping a low profile because I felt guilty about something, because I was the one who should be receiving the lashes of the cane, not Anil. It is curious, I can remember the colour of the earth at the camp, and the way it gave off that acrid dust, I can remember the rain, I can remember the mountain at the end of the camp, beyond the stream, the dark shape that stood out against the sky at night and blocked our view of the stars. I can remember all this, but I cannot remember what I had done that day for which Anil took such a beating.

As a child I was a weakling. Of the three brothers I was the one who was the most fearful, the one who was always somewhat sickly, the one they protected the most from the dust, the rain, the mud. And yet it was I who survived at Mapou.

Among our many tasks at the camp the one we never baulked at was fetching the water. The stream flowed past a few hundred yards away from the camp and we knew that, unlike the other children at the camp, we were lucky. Some of them went with their fathers to the cane fields, others had to dig and maintain ditches to drain away the water in anticipation of the next deluge, whereas we went to the stream.

At the edge of the camp there was a little wood we would walk through on a path scarcely marked among the thickets. Anil led the way, Vinod brought up the rear, I was, once again, the most protected of the three. This path seemed to me marvellous. Along the way there were wild strawberries and in summer mulberries grew plump on the bushes. Butterflies came and settled quite close to us, we would stop and look at them, filled with wonder at their mixture of colours, and I am certain that at such moments what each of us dreamed of was turning into a butterfly: arraying himself in bright colours, becoming weightless and flying away.

Anil always walked with a stick bent near the top into a U, sometimes resting his hand in the crook of it. It was a branch from a camphor tree which had been strongly scented for a while but had then simply become a little boy's stick. He would twitch the grasses in front of him to drive away the snakes, which terrified us, Vinod and me. Anil adored this stick. It was, after all, the only thing which was really his own, which he did not have to share with anyone at all. It was a source neither of danger nor envy and no-one could claim it from him.

We could hear the stream even before we saw it and at this moment Anil would sometimes turn to us with a mild smile and I would restrain myself from leaping and running. We would go there at a time of day when we were certain not to meet anyone. It was a stream that flowed down from the mountain and even when I was little I was aware of the purity of its water which emerged from the higher slopes, perhaps from the clouds, it was dazzlingly clear and, according to Vinod, had a faintly sugary taste. This stream was our Eden and we travelled from the hell of our camp to paradise almost every day by way of the little wood, passing through it with ceremony.

The three of us had six buckets to fill and we would delay the moment when we had to return to the camp. We caught little fish trying to swim against the current and peered at ourselves in the water. And today, when I think of my brothers, I see our three faces reflected in the stream, blurred a little by the ripples on the surface of the water: Anil on my left, Vinod on my right, and we appear startlingly alike, with our crudely trimmed black hair, our eyes swollen from the dust, our thin necks and our teeth which look too big for us, so hollow are our cheeks, and the way we have, all three of us, of taking it in turns to look at one another and laugh.

Anil was the one who signalled our departure and we never argued. We filled the buckets to the brim and began the return journey, which was much less pleasant than the outward one. Anil had taught us how to walk with a supple tread so as to spill as little water as possible. The iron handles cut into the palms of our hands and we clenched our teeth. Anil tucked his stick under his arm and never dropped it.

When my mother returned from work the house had to have been cleaned, the earth in front of the door tamped down as neatly as possible, the water must be in the barrel, the wood lined up for the fire, the bundles of dried leaves well fastened and ourselves seated there, as good as gold. Night would fall quickly, the men would come home from the fields and then another life would begin for ourselves and for our poor mother, one filled with shouting, the stench of alcohol and tears.

All the men in the camp drank, I have no idea where or how they bought this drink because no-one had enough to eat. We swallowed flat bread baked by our mothers and fried herbs, occasionally vegetables, and every day we drank stewed tea. My father was no better or worse than the others. He yelled things we could not understand, sang songs which were incomprehensible, so heavy and swollen with alcohol was his tongue, and if we did not sing the way he wanted he would hit us. Often we ended up outside, huddled against our mother, and we were not the only family in this situation.

What more can be said about those nights in the camp? I did not feel I was any more unhappy than the others, my universe began and ended there. To me, this was how the world was, with fathers who worked from dawn till dusk, came home drunk and bullied their families.

In the year I was six my father sent me to school. Only four children from the camp went there and for us, the three brothers, school, along with the stream and the steam from the factory, was another aspect of paradise. But my father had decided to send only myself, neither Anil, nor Vinod, and this was the worst of punishments for me. I wept, I wailed, I shouted, I was impervious to strokes from the cane, to my father's slaps and threats and, above all, I was unmoved by my mother's pleading. She looked at me with moist eyes and said to me Raj, I ask you, do it for me, go to the school.

In those days children never won. I did indeed go to the school. There were only two classes, one for the little ones, the beginners, like me, and the other for the ones who, in theory, could read, write and do sums. They gave me a slate on which I could write with chalk and I must confess that, when I encountered this unknown world of school and teaching, my immense distress was diminished. I set off at seven o'clock in the morning and my two brothers would come with me to the edge of the camp, at the opposite end from the mountain. I had to walk round the camp, since the classrooms were located some way away from the factory. Sometimes, for as long as this walk lasted, a good half hour, I would imagine that all three of us were on our way to school and that soon the cards on which the world was explained to us in pictures and words would be displayed before all our eyes. On one of them there was a man dressed in trousers and a short-sleeved shirt, he had wavy black hair, a gentle face and a smile. At the bottom of the card the word, PAPA. Then Anil and Vinod would have been able to believe what I told them: not all the fathers in the world were like the ones at the camp, like our own.

My brothers would contrive to wait for me in the afternoon so we could go to the stream together, but often I would come back to an empty camp and all its ugliness would suddenly become apparent to me. At such moments there was only one thing I wanted to do: to bury my head in my hands and weep. I compared it to the card for HOUSE, a lovely, clean, white thing, with a blue roof, proof against rain, it was solid, truly solid, with proper walls. It was clear that in houses like this the dust did not swirl round people's faces like a cloud of flies, the mud did not slither viciously, like snakes, into every nook and cranny. It was clear that in houses like this there was not a bamboo cane, all ribs and knots, with a very fine tip, propped up against the wall, motionless, innocent, harmless but daring you to look at it.

At school I also learned a sense of guilt. That insidious thing which held me back from being an ordinary little boy, roaring with laughter, playing with the others, or just sitting quietly, staring in front of me. When I was in the classroom this feeling left me. But after the lesson was over I once more became Raj, the only brother who goes to school. Why me? I never ceased to ask myself. In my bag made of dried palm leaves I always hid the dried pear handed out at the morning break, but the cow's milk they gave us had to be drunk then and there. I drank it slowly, closing my eyes, thinking hard about Anil and Vinod, picturing them cleaning the house, cutting wood, tying up cane leaves, bent, weary. All they had to make them grow was sugared water.

I wished my father had chosen another of his sons to educate. But Anil would soon be going out with him every morning to cut sugar cane, he was strong, he already had muscles that bulged beneath his skin, he never complained and, with his determination and strength at work, he would earn money, coins he would not drown in arrack, but would give ceremoniously to my mother. Vinod would have been better in my place, but he was nimble and clever and, though he did not have Anil's strength in his arms and legs, he was lively and never complained either. Whereas I was not much use for anything, since I spent half the year coughing, half the year drinking bitter herbal decoctions to get rid of the loose cough that lingered within me, my mother said, and sometimes I was in the grip of convulsions for whole nights and my feet became frozen. When the cough finally calmed down I would trail along with my brothers, feeling as if there were something gnawing at my chest. My legs lacked muscles, they were thin as sticks of bamboo, and I was such a light thing that Anil often carried me. I would wrap my two legs round his belly, my arms round his neck, and he settled me on his back and great was my love for him.

When I came back from school and everything had been done without me, my sense of guilt made me hyperactive. I would rush about searching for fresh sugar cane leaves for the kitchen hearth, even if my brothers had already stacked up the bundle behind the house. I wanted to go and fetch more water, but the barrel would not hold more than six bucketfuls. I tamped down the earth again and when the wind made the dust motes dance I stayed in the house, armed with a rag, chasing away the grit as it settled on my mother's cooking utensils, on our sleeping mats and even on my father's bamboo cane, all ribs and knots, with its long, fine tip. Coughing away, I struggled against the monster inside me that always won in the end, I was out of breath, my arms throbbed with pain but never mind, as I flailed about like a weary madman, I made my brothers laugh.

Our life of mud and grit came to an end shortly after New Year's Day 1944. At the year's end we had received clothes given by the wives of the bosses at the sugar factory. Clothes already worn by their children, but this did not matter at all to us, we were thrilled by the fabrics, the colours and the styles. We all three of us had white shirts as well as shorts of different sizes and colours. Mine were a green pair, made of a soft material and if I ran my fingers over it I could feel the strands in the fabric that were not visible to the naked eye. The shirt made my neck itch. Anil had a kind of Bermuda shorts, I know this now, but I remember we were forever making fun of him, his calves emerged from this long, khaki affair and at the time we thought it was too big for him. We only knew about shorts and trousers, not Bermuda shorts. Vinod had a pair of dark brown shorts which my mother took in at the waist with three safety-pins. We were probably ridiculous, but we felt, how shall I say? Special.

We went on wearing these clothes for several weeks and we had them on when we went to the stream that afternoon. The shirts no longer made us feel itchy, they were dirty, and only one of the safety-pins on Vinod's shorts had survived. After weeks of intense heat the clouds were low and dark, and half the mountain was hidden. Not a single butterfly came to meet us, the bushes were dry, the wind set off miniature tornadoes and we stopped to watch the leaves spiralling up and falling again. We heard the stream quite late and my big brother turned back and smiled at us, but we did not hurry as we usually did.

The stream was pure and clear, with a faintly sugary taste, as Vinod would say. At the height of summer it became narrow and had difficulty in making its way round the great rocks, grey with sunlight, that crowded into its bed. We played there for a moment then Anil decided to climb upstream towards the mountain, to find a place where the water gushed out more powerfully. I remember glancing at the camp. Merely a rapid glance over my shoulder, the trees we had just been passing through looked undernourished and were dancing at the mercy of the wind. We moved on, our buckets in our hands, Anil in front with his stick, Vinod behind me, and it was at the foot of the mountain that the rain suddenly came down.

I am seventy today and I still remember, as if it were yesterday, how the thunder felt as if it were coming from our own stomachs, so much did it reverberate within us. I remember the fear, at the start, the eerie silence that followed the thunder, which petrified everything. Nature itself was on hold, and, as for us, we no longer dared move. Long minutes when huge, cool raindrops began by wetting our hair and our faces, then soaked our clothes. I remember the ghostly mist that arose from the earth when this had absorbed the first drops. We generally enjoyed such a moment but this time it was different. I sensed it, my brothers sensed it. Very quickly lightning flashes were unleashed, more thunderclaps rang out and we began to run.

How long did we spend hurtling downhill? The dry pebbles, which moments before had been grazing our feet, had disappeared, we were treading on slippery, sticky soil, struggling to pluck our feet from it. The sun had gone out. There were walls of rain and a curtain of sulphur arose from the earth. Anil's white shirt bobbed up and down in front of me and I was trying not to let this fragment of white out of my sight. He was saying come on come on come on and then suddenly, in the blink of an eye, nothing more. No voice, no shirt in front of me. I stopped and Vinod bumped into me. My little brother gripped my arm and began calling Anil Anil Anil. I did the same, together we yelled out our elder brother's name, I do not know how long we went on shouting like that, running through the mud, without any landmark, our eyes closed by the force of the wind and the rain and soon, heaven help me, soon there was only my voice shouting Anil Anil, and then Anil, Vinod, Anil, Vinod. I yelled with all my might but the wind, the rain, the thunder, the flashes of lightning, the roaring of the torrent of mud that our beloved stream had turned into drowned my voice and gave me no chance.

Five days later the men of the camp found Vinod, without his shirt, his head trapped behind a rock. It is not easy, when you are a child of eight, to see your little brother, who loved you more than anything in the world, his head smashed in by who knows what, his fingers and toes torn off by the stones hurtling down the mountainside, his body battered from having remained trapped behind a rock for five days, at the mercy of a stream we so loved, the stream which, for him, had a faintly sugary taste and which had become a torrent of mud, loose stones and rocks. He was cremated the same day, all the preparations for the ceremony appeared as if by magic: the stretcher of camphor wood, the white sheet, the garlands of flowers, the incense, the priest with a big red spot on his forehead and his book of sacred verses in his hands.

Anil's body was never found. A few days later, in the course of one last search with the people from the camp, I discovered his stick. It was there at the edge of the little wood and I recognized it, thanks to its U-shaped end. I let it lie in my hand and I could never express how much I missed my elder brother at that moment. The stream had become limpid and pure once more and while the men were searching for Anil's body, I tossed his stick into the current. I do not know why I did that, it was an unpremeditated gesture, but it was, as I have said, the only thing that truly belonged to my elder brother. The stick floated downstream, catching several times against rocks, but then it, too, disappeared. I leaned over towards the mirror of the water, as in the old days, and saw only a single furrowed face, with bulging eyes and a grimace. A bottomless well opened up within me and I know I did not hurl myself into that solitary image, into that thin, unhappy reflection so as to obliterate it, I know I did not do this because my mother came running up behind me, calling out my name at the top of her voice, calling the only son who was left to her.

We remained precisely three more days in the camp at Mapou. One morning, as dawn was beginning to tinge the mountain with blue and the sky was gently lighting up, my mother took me by the hand and we followed my father towards Beau-Bassin. I did not look back at Mapou, the camp, the little wood which lay between it and the stream, the cane fields, the tall stone chimney, the cushion of white steam, nor did I weep, but inside my head I could still hear the ear-splitting roar I had been trying to cover with my voice. Anil, Vinod, Anil, Vinod.

3

WE TRAVELLED HALFWAY ACROSS THE ISLAND, from the north to the centre. I imagine that on the long road to Beau-Bassin we must have ridden in carts pulled by oxen or donkeys, perhaps we took a train, for they existed at that time, we walked, we slept in the open air, we saw locomotives, people, landscapes, flowers, gleaming horses, earth tracks which petered out at the sea's edge, the sea itself, perhaps, well-marked roads, houses and mountains whose existence we had never dreamed of, we who had never left Mapou. Despite my best efforts I can remember nothing. Did I cling to my mother, did she hold my hand, did she weep for her sons, for her home, for the community of the wretched of the earth whom we were leaving behind? What was my father doing during all this time, he whose hands were no longer busy cutting canes, chopping off their heads crowned with the volatile white flowers that had blinded so many workers in the fields, what was he doing with his bare, horny hands, freed from the strips of cloth he wrapped them in, to give them makeshift protection against thorns, bark, stings and splinters? What did he do with his mouth which, for the length of this endless journey no longer had the taste of arrack in it, no longer numbed by this heavy, bitter alcohol, what did he do with his hoarse voice without the songs of the fields, the camp, his songs of misfortune and his workers' laments? What did this man do, cut loose and adrift on this journey with what remained of his family, without the green bamboo cane, all ribs and knots, that he used to crack against our bodies? And what about me, timid and frail, without my two brothers? This journey could have united us even more, nourished hopes of bright new dawns, we could have been pioneers, people might have spoken of us with admiration, the first family to leave Mapou entirely of their own free will, because we wanted something better, refusing to believe all the tales that said this was our destiny: rain, mud, dust and poverty. But no, we were simply a family at our wits' end, poleaxed by immense grief, and so we fled.

I never asked my mother how my father got the job at the Beau-Bassin prison. I believe she knew no more than I did, they were not like modern couples who tell one another everything, who discuss the smallest decisions, bound together by their secrets, my parents were not like that.

If someone other than myself were telling this story, someone who could see all this from above, he would surely claim that at Beau-Bassin we were better off. The earth beneath our feet was a fine, rich, brown colour. You could sow vegetables and flowers in it and the roots of the trees that grew there were deeply embedded, with no sharp, black rocks to bar their way. The leaves on these trees were broad, gleaming and green. Among the leaves grew white and pink buds, which later turned into fruits. Mangoes, lychees, longans, guavas, pawpaws, which I ate slowly, always thinking of my brothers. Breadfruit trees, jackfruit trees, avocado trees, which offered fruits all the year round, green or ripe, savoury or sweet. Vines upon the ground concealed cucumbers, squashes and courgettes, there were velvety bushes which produced tomatoes, pimentos and aubergines. Beneath the ground, potatoes, carrots, beetroot and sweet potatoes ripened. Sunlight and rain were now essential, pleasant and gentle things, nothing like those monsters at Mapou, which overturn the earth, get into your stomach, crush your heart and kill children.

Our house at Beau-Bassin was sunk deep in woodland as one might nowadays picture a forest warden's house or a hunting lodge. Later on my mother told me that nobody wanted this house. It was midway between the prison and the cemetery and people used to say it was the dwelling-place of lost souls. My mother giggled like a girl when she told me this but I was glad she only shared this confidence with me when I was already a strong, fully grown adult and such tales no longer frightened me.

I should like to recall the first days at Beau-Bassin as clearly as I remember my first years at Mapou, but even if I concentrate, I can only call to mind a series of pictures, as if scattered through a book with no words, no title. The house walls overgrown with creepers as thick as bamboos – though you would not think so to look at them like this – making elegant patterns. My parents and myself tearing these creepers down with all our strength, because they were infested with ants and lizards. The bare walls of the house, covered in a thick grey-green skin. The presence of the forest all around the house and the solemn atmosphere it gave off, the green colour it lent everything, the deep silence around us. My mother's lips moving rapidly as she prepared decoctions and mixtures which she would then sprinkle along the threshold and the window-ledges. And next day, the rats lying there, the hedgehogs with jaws agape, the limp snakes we found. My mother's hand working the pestle, crushing, pounding, annihilating the enemies. My father's eyes on me, that look of his growing darker and darker. At whom could he yell, whom could he beat to exorcize his rage? And the question on the tip of his tongue, the question he was never able to utter out loud but which I heard every time I passed close by him, every time his hand fell upon me, upon my mother. Why you? Why you, Raj, – you weak little good-for-nothing, why did you survive? Why you? Why you?

I remember spending long minutes after I woke up searching for my brothers' eyes, the endless time that elapsed before I came to my senses and realized that I was now forever alone, remembering Vinod's trapped head and Anil's stick thrown into the stream back there at Mapou.

Pictures of those new mornings when, instead of binding his feet and hands with strips of fabric, my father put on brown trousers and a beige shirt to go to work. The soap he lathered over his face and his hair flattened down with great smacks of his wetted palms. The silhouette of this new man attired in his uniform in the doorway and the way he had of walking, his legs a bit apart, as if the fabric were itchy or because he wanted to crease his trousers as little as possible. The feeling I had when my father set off for his new work – his job of "prison warder", as he used to say, with an almost imperceptible upward movement of his head, a subtle straightening of his back and his eyes opened wider – the feeling, as he walked away from the house, that the forest was going to swallow him up entirely and that he would never return, lost in the woodland maze.

During those days spent all alone at Beau-Bassin, immersed in that somehow muted light, which now took on the colour of the forest, now the colour of the flowers my mother had planted around the house to create a benign ring, or else that of the bluish mountains in the distance, I discovered a taste for hiding-places. I would lie low in corners, tucking my feet and legs in underneath me, I would climb up into trees and crouch in the forks of branches, my body coiled in on itself like a snake, I would dig holes beneath the squash plants in the vegetable garden and crawl in there, with my belly to the ground, my hands buried in the earth up to my wrists, my face hidden among the creepers. I would remain for hours like that, motionless, listening to my own breathing, being no more than a heart beating as softly as possible. It was only when I was hidden, squeezed in, tucked away, that I was calm, that I was more or less at ease. Outside there were too many new things for my solitary self and I should have liked to be able to share the abundance of this calm, blue sky, the profusion of the forest's deep, unending green and, above all, the silence which spread like the sea, creeping in everywhere, into the house, behind my father, around my mother, by day, by night, a tangible silence which was the foundation upon which my little decimated family now rested.

Sometimes my father shattered this silence, I would hear him yelling in the distance and my mother would draw close to me, just as surely as my father's footfalls and voice were drawing closer to the house and we would wait for his hand to come hammering down beside us, beside me, upon me, upon my mother. At such times I was sure the whole forest was listening to us, all that green, the dense mass of foliage and timber that used to alarm me so much during the first weeks, was focusing on the din we made as it rent the night at Beau-Bassin.

These woods were a combination of eucalypts, mangoes, camphor trees, ebony trees and tropical almonds, and at the age of eight I could never have imagined that one day all of this would exist only in my memory, the dense greenery, the scents of damp earth, cut wood, moss and rotting fruit. Oh, the fear I had the first few times I walked through them, those woods of my childhood, and later the pride I took in knowing the tracks, the paths to take, the traps, the lairs, better than anyone. I could run right through the trees with my eyes shut, I knew when you had to swerve to avoid the big mango, slow down on the left near the almond, on account of the roots which would cunningly trip you, duck beneath the forked and broken branches of the eucalyptus, make a great leap, without pausing, without stopping to think just beside the other mango, where the mangoes smelled of turpentine, because there was a hole there and beside the hole an anthill with great red ants which have shiny round bottoms, ones that give you giant blisters and excruciating bites.

Today I like to think that if those woods still existed – for in fact they no longer do, in their place there are modern blocks of flats with potted plants at the windows and balconies on which families sit staring at who knows what – I could still retrace that path. Now as I think back to all that, for the first time in many years, you know I swear I get itchy feet and old reflexes come to life in my scrawny muscles. Turn left, straight ahead, here we go, head down, swing on a branch, take a run at it, grit your teeth, be like an animal, a tiger, something that is afraid of nothing.

In Beau-Bassin I went to school, too, and there is

not a lot I can say on the subject. I was aware of being one of the poorest in the class, with clothes so old they were wearing thin, becoming transparent. I did not play with anyone; I ate the lunch my mother had prepared for me each morning and stayed in the classroom. I thought a lot about my brothers when I saw all the children playing and shouting and if the other lads called out to me sometimes, I would hold back, say no and bow my head and the children would whisper amongst themselves, they used to say I was very sick and playing might kill me. In truth, they were not wrong. I was sick for my brothers and I felt sure that if I played with the others, laughed, joined in their games, I should be betraying them, alienating myself from them for ever. I stayed in my corner and talked to myself, very softly. That, too, was something I had learned to do at Beau-Bassin. I told myself stories, as I would once have told stories to Anil and Vinod. I moved my lips as my mother did when she was pounding her potions, her herbs, to ward off the evil eye, mischief and the vermin that came to eat the vegetables in the kitchen garden and nibble the ends of our toes.

My teacher was called Mademoiselle Elsa and when she put her white hand on my shoulder I felt a ball of warmth swelling in my stomach like a balloon. My little Raj, she would say. When on the very rare occasions my mother came to fetch me from school Mademoiselle Elsa would come out to see her, and tell her that I was a good boy, I would certainly go far, I learned quickly, I had caught up after being behind, I was one of the best at French and English and that soon, perhaps, I could put my name down to take the exam for the scholarship, that famous scholarship, which gives you a place at the best high school and money for books, and you still have some left to buy food, oh yes, she was convinced I could have all that. My mother listened to her wide-eyed, and afterwards on the way home she said very little to me, as usual – my mother rarely talked much now since we had left Mapou – but she gripped my hand tightly all the way to the house. In those days her heart probably knew nothing beyond the sadness of having lost two children on the same day, but when Mademoiselle Elsa was talking to her, looking her straight in the eye, I like to think that she held herself more erect, that some strength came and flowed into her fingers and that the only child who was left to her afforded her a little pride.

When my mother died her belongings were contained in three suitcases, one of which was entirely devoted to myself and her grandson. She, who would never have sent me to school had it not been for my father, had preserved in it all my early school exercise books, as well as those of my son, copies of our exam certificates and also our old school satchels, and I believe that, just as other people like showing photographs of their family, their houses, their cars, my mother liked to open this suitcase to show to guests. I remember she would sometimes leaf through my notebooks with unfeigned admiration, turning the pages, as if this were a precious legacy, and when I passed my exams she took my hands in hers and tears came to her eyes. With my son, too, she was attentive, tidying his desk, arranging his books and notebooks according to thickness and size, sharpening his pencils to perfection, and every evening my poor boy was awarded a milky brew which was believed, as my mother herself put it, to "feed the brain".

Up until the holidays in 1944 I had never seen the prison where my father worked. He had once told me that there were dangerous people in that prison, runaways, robbers, bad men. My father gripped me by the shoulders in telling me this because he knew I ran about in the forest and hid in the trees and he wanted to frighten me, so he stressed the "A"s, "E"s, "O"s and "U"s in the words he was saying, shaking me all the while. His mouth and eyes opened wide at the same time, as if driven by a mechanism inside him and when I saw him setting off in his uniform each morning I wanted more than anything to follow him and watch him locking up the dAngerous ones, the rUnaways, the rObbers and the bAd mEn, in his great prison.

My prayer was to be answered. During the holidays at the end of the year, at midday from Monday to Saturday, my mother made me take my father's lunch to him at work. I skirted the forest, turned left a little before the earth road that led to the village and followed the prison wall up to the gate. I waited there a while and my father would come hurrying up. I would hand him his lunch, still hot, through the bars and he would invariably say to me, be off with you, go home.

Of course, I paid no attention. The very first day I followed the wall, which was so high it gave me a headache, with my eyes firmly on my sandals, for I was convinced that he would swoop down on me. At the corner I branched off, skirted right round the prison, and came back to the gate from the other side, where the ground rose a little and where, in place of the wall, there was a high barbed-wire fence. And there I found the best hiding-place of my life. A hiding-place where I could let my heart slow down, my life come to a standstill and observe the dAngerous ones, the rUnaways, the rObbers and the bAd mEn.

4

I WAS HIDDEN IN A BUSH, WITH THE LEAVES crackling a little beneath me and twigs sticking into my thighs that would leave scratches of dried blood, and what I saw, as I hid there, was nothing like what I had imagined.

I was expecting to see cages, fences, padlocks and policemen. I had pictured shouting, dogs, and men with yellow eyes, which would be the dangerous prisoners, the runaways, robbers and bad men. I also formed a clear picture of my father in his uniform at the centre of all this, with all these people going in fear of him, as my mother and I dreaded him when he came home drunk in the evening and his hand came hammering down beside us, upon us, upon my mother, upon me.

There was no-one in the compound. In this prison, with its blue and white sign, like one for an amusement park, *Welcome to the State Prison of Beau-Bassin*, perfect calm reigned. True, I could only see a part of it from my hiding-place. To my left, lower down, was the gate through which I had handed my father's lunch, then a huge mango tree, hidden by the wall from anyone looking at the prison on the other side. It was probably the largest mango tree I have ever seen, with a massive trunk, and smooth red fruits which stood out against the lush, green foliage, hanging heavily, ready to fall. Beneath the tree, a broad shady area, never penetrated by the sun, gave shelter to three stools, carefully arranged. Then there was a house, like the ones on my picture cards at school. With a canopy almost covered in mauve bougainvilleas, a verandah, wooden balustrades, windows with shutters and curtains. Beside the house a pathway led into the depths of the prison and although the sun was at its height I could not see a great deal. Against the wall on the right there was a line of cabins each made of red or blue corrugated iron, and these shelters, like the pathway, continued right into the heart of the prison.

This first image of the prison at Beau-Bassin is imprinted on my mind, as sleek and unmoving as a picture postcard. There was not so much as a cat in the compound, no sound, no wind even, it seemed to me, and it was as if someone had staged the whole thing for my benefit, knowing I was going to come and hide there. Just beyond the double barbed-wire fence – and if I stretched out my arm I could touch the point of one of the twists of wire – there were bushes with wild flowers, then a strip of lush, green grass and pots with gardenias, marguerite daisies and roses.

It made a great impression on me to see it, this kind of tranquil splendour where, what is more, my father worked. Today it is a recollection which disgusts me somewhat, a big lie I believed in for a time, since this semblance of ease – the billowing curtains, the fruits, the flowers, the lawn, the silence – was only a façade, it was all just for show, and if one probed just a little, darkness, squalor, cries and tears were all there to be uncovered.

I think that if I had been an ordinary boy with no history – by this I mean a boy who had not spent the first years of his life in a ramshackle hut, who had not lost both his brothers on the same day, a boy who had friends to play with and did not hide in holes dug in the bare earth or on the branches of trees, a boy who did not talk to himself for hours on end, a boy who, when he shut his eyes at night, saw something other than his little brother's body trapped beneath a rock – I would not have stayed there long, this bizarre prison would have bored me. But I was Raj and I liked dark corners and places where nothing stirred. And so I remained like that for a very long while, watching the prison, sweeping it assiduously with my gaze, from left to right, from right to left and so on. I told myself that the next time Mademoiselle Elsa asked us what we would like to do when we grew older – a question which, so far, I had never known how to answer, the words "grow older" would brutally remind me of my older brother, Anil, and so this question always brought tears to my eyes and started a fit of coughing, just like at Mapou – I should say that I should like a job where you can hide and keep watch.

Suddenly a bell rang and I saw my father emerging from behind the mango tree, as if he had been hiding there all the time, and settling himself against the gate, where the chains met, with several padlocks to hold them fast. Three policemen emerged from the house with the bougainvilleas, and walked down the front steps. They were real policeman, not at all like my father, with his brown uniform, who now looked rather pale, thin and, above all, timid. The real policemen were taller, had navy-blue trousers, white shirts, blue and white caps and, importantly, truncheons at their belts. From where I was it looked as if they all had stiff black tails. They stationed themselves nonchalantly around the house, along the pathway that led into the depths of the prison, quite unlike my father, who stood tensed against the gate, it was hard to tell if he was trying to break the padlocks with his bare hands or to guard them against everything and everyone. After several minutes, from the precise spot where my father had materialized, pale shadowy figures appeared. A line of people, very thin, dragging their feet in silence, slowly following the earth footpath, then spreading out across the compound. Men, women, children. All white people. Their clothes were too big for them, too long, dirty and ragged, there was something odd about the way they were dressed and they looked a little like ghosts. I had never seen white people so thin and weary – at the age of eight I thought white people were bosses at the factory, drove about in cars and flew aircraft, I should never have believed they could be locked up. They stayed in the compound, hardly stirring, perhaps this was a kind of freedom they were granted, but the sun made them screw their eyes up, they hunched their shoulders as you do when going out in the rain, they gazed at the sky, shading their eyes, and many of them took shelter beneath the mango tree or under the canopy, but I remember that not one of them sat down on the three wooden stools, even though they looked exhausted. Nobody made any gesture, not even to pick a mango to satisfy their hunger or quench their thirst. I remember the tree's dense foliage and the abundant fruits that hung there, looking in the distance like spots of deep red, and these pale, sickly people lingering underneath, as if they had not the slightest idea of what was above their heads. I did not understand what I was seeing, I could not begin to believe that these were they, the dAngerous ones, rUnaways, rObbers and bAd mEn. Apart from their colour, they looked just as worn out as my mother, staring in front of them as my mother sometimes used to – she would focus on a spot, whether it be night or day, and turn into a statue. I reflected that perhaps these people, too, had suddenly lost sons, just like that, for no reason, in a way which left them unable to give vent to their anger or accuse anyone.

I cannot remember the precise moment when I noticed David. Perhaps it was when he walked towards the barbed wire. What I saw first was his hair, that magnificent mop of it, which floated around his head but which was certainly his and his alone, in a way that nothing has ever belonged to me, those curls hiding his brow, and his way of advancing stiffly, not limping, for all the world as if he were made of wood and iron and his machinery had not been oiled for quite some while. He had brown shorts on, like my little brother, Vinod, and this emphasized the whiteness of his legs. He came up to the fence, slowly, without hurrying, and it seemed to me quite incredible that he should be doing this when he was in prison, as if he were strolling in his own garden and he drew closer and closer, there now, I could see his face better, the tiny face of a blond child lost amid the humid heat of Beau-Bassin. There were other children in the compound, but they mainly stayed clinging to an adult, no-one was playing, no-one was running, no-one seemed to be speaking. Every one a little Raj, like me.

David told me later that he was going to look at the wild flowers which grew near to the barbed wire. David adored flowers, it was as if he had never seen any in his life before, but it is true that the flowers at Beau-Bassin are different from those that grow in Prague. At the time I was convinced he was coming towards me. His eyes were fixed on mine, nothing else could be possible and my heart began to race. He came closer and closer to the fence, I was shaking, I huddled deeper into the earth, then suddenly he turned back towards the others with a few puppet-like steps. He stood there like that, with his back to me, he was at most a few yards away from me. His shirt was torn so that the sleeves clung to his shoulders and his wrists and I could see the backs of his arms. He sat down on the thick grass and did like me, he looked from left to right, from right to left. I could not take my eyes off his hair, it was probably one of the most beautiful things I had ever seen at my young age. In the brilliant sun of that December day, a few weeks before the end of the year, barely two months before the anniversary of my brothers' deaths, his blond crown shone like a cluster of golden threads. It was magnificent. When he turned his head back and forth to keep watch – just like me, yes, even without knowing one another we did the same things – his locks bounced gently, as if they were mounted on thousands of tiny springs.

I was very pleased with my day, with my hiding-place, with my discoveries, I should once have been eager to tell Vinod and Anil all about it, as I used to with what I learned at school, and their eyes would open wide, those eyes that resembled mine, what a joy it was for me to tell them things that made their eyes open wide, now all this was just for me, and that was why I talked to myself, to recount something about my day, to pour out some of the words, the emotions, the pictures, the feelings that were piling up inside me.

Suddenly David's curls began to shake, his shoulders too, and he buried his face between his knees, which he had brought up against his chest as he sat down. Then I heard him crying. I knew it only too well, this sobbing that racks you, that makes you softly murmur oh, oh, as if someone were slowly, very slowly, plunging a knife into your heart. I knew it only too well, the sobbing that suddenly surges up from nowhere, just as you are sitting peacefully on a lush, green lawn with the warm sun on your shoulders. I straightened up, with a terrible desire to call out to him, to comfort him, to say to him, as Anil used to say to me, don't cry, it'll be alright, you've got a runny nose and, yuk, you're swallowing snot. It always made us laugh when he said that, you're swallowing snot, and then he would add, it tastes salty doesn't it? And a moment later the tears were forgotten.

Then that day I did what David had done, it was something that happened to me from time to time, a knot suddenly tightening in the pit of my stomach, finding it hard to breathe and tears welling up, which I was powerless to resist. I buried my head in the leaves and wept, as he was doing just a few yards away from me.

I do not know how long I kept my face pressed into the earth, but suddenly I heard a shout from my father. He said something like, hey, you there! I looked up and was amazed to see that David was clinging to the fence, the spikes on the barbed wire may even have been going into his hands. He was staring at my hiding-place. I lifted my neck, my face must have looked alarming, tears, earth, leaves clinging to it, but he smiled at me. I tried to return his smile, my tears had stopped abruptly, that knot in my stomach had loosened, but I simply looked at him with bulging red eyes and the head of a savage. He went on smiling at me. Then I gave a kind of little wave with my hand and behind him I saw a policeman approaching. I lay low once more and David turned round. The policeman made an abrupt gesture, as if to say, get down from there and, as another bell rang out and all the thin, dirty, weary people plunged into the sunless pathway, abandoning their own places of shelter under the mango tree or the canopy, the policeman came right up to the fence and stared in my direction. Then he made a kind of clicking sound with dry lips, a somewhat weary "chik", and went off.

And there in the dark shadows of the pathway which led them to an unknown place, the place they were all going to now, shuffling their feet, moving fatalistically, as if there were nothing else to do, there in the dark shadows the glow of David's golden hair faded, as the sunlight gradually left it.

5

THAT EVENING MY FATHER CAME HOME WITH mangoes. Even as my mother was still cooking for five, he had brought five mangoes. I peered at their undersides, as if these smooth red fruits, dotted with little green shards, as if they could know exactly how I had spent my afternoon. I had seen them poised and dangling there amid the dense foliage and I felt sure they must remember me too. When I took one in my hand it was heavy and warm.

My father took out his little knife and sat down on the flat stone in front of the house facing the forest. Slowly and meticulously he cut out a thin slice of mango, held it between his fingers and the knife and sucked it in. The gleaming orange slice slipped noiselessly into his mouth and he gulped it down without chewing. I do not know where he had learned to do that, in the old days at Mapou we used to crouch down, eating our mangoes with both hands, with the juice trickling down our forearms, quickly catching it with our tongues. In the old days at Mapou we ate the whole mango, the skin, the little, rather hard tip that had held it to the branch and we sucked the stone for a long, long time until it was rough and insipid, good only to throw on the fire.

I walked a few steps around the house, the heat had died down and the silence of the forest formed a thick shield about us. I went up to my father, running the tip of my tongue over the questions I wanted to put to him. Who were those people, those white prisoners? Were they Beau-Bassin's bad men, robbers and runaways? Why did they walk so slowly, as if they had nothing left in their legs, just skin and a bit of bone? And those thin, sickly children, had they stolen too, or done things that get you put in prison? My father did not invite me to sit beside him, nor did he look at me, he went on staring straight ahead, turning his little knife over in his fingers, and stood up with a sigh.

Long after this, when I became a father and loved my son in a way I had not known my heart was capable of, when I took my son in my arms, an action my body and arms performed even before I was aware of it, I never ceased to ask myself what it would have cost my father to look at me normally without his madman's menacing stare, perhaps just once to invite me to sit beside him, to tell me a few things about his day, or to say nothing, simply to share a moment of silence in the darkness, what would that have cost him?

But in those days when my father was like that, distant and cold, I used to thank god, as my mother had taught me to do, for every peaceful night, for every evening when he came home sober, silent, inoffensive, his heart as hard and flat as the stone on which he sat after supper. I did not put my questions to him that night, before going to bed I thanked god for his great kindness, for his great mercy in giving us an evening without a father hammering down his hand, his feet, beside us, beside my mother, upon my mother, upon me.

During the following weeks I daily took my father's lunch to the prison at noon. My days were filled and I could no longer wander about in the forest as much as before. For some time my mother had been helping the village dressmaker, Madame Ghislaine, who lived in a dazzlingly white house. All around the house she had planted red dahlias and it was a fine sight, the flowers nestling up against the wall, red against white, like inseparable brothers and sisters. My mother was helping her out for the new year and was adding what she herself called "the finishing touches": sewing a hem with fine stitches, adding flounces, gathering a waistband with regular pleats, trimming off all the loose threads, starching, ironing, folding. During those holidays my mother would send me early in the morning to fetch dresses, skirts, corsets, petticoats, trousers. I had to take the track behind our house, walk for a good half-hour and the first house at the start of the village was Madame Ghislaine's, all white with its red trimmings. The dressmaker would put the clothes into a sheet, and gather up the sides into the middle with a big knot. Then she helped me settle this large bundle on to my back and, as if it were quite normal for a puny lad like me to cope with a weight like this on his shoulders, she returned swiftly to her black sewing machine.

Grasping the big knot with both hands over my shoulder, I would climb back up the long road to my home. The sheet would slither about and I would have to give it a heave with my hips to hitch the bundle up again and get a new grip on the knot. There was no stopping, I should have had to put the sheet down on the ground and it would have got dirty. I was really afraid of dropping that sheet and the dresses, skirts, corsets, petticoats and trousers being strewn over the ground, so that, just like my father, my mother, too, would begin to regret that it was me, Raj, who had survived. Anil would have had no problem carrying that bundle, he was so strong, and Vinod would have devised a better method of balancing the weight on his back and would have carried it with a smile, as he used to when he was burdened with two quaking buckets filled to the brim with water.

It was a long trek that I made, with my back hunched and soon burning hot, my knees bent, my arms and fingers weak, as if all their strength had drained away, but I never dropped my mother's livelihood. When I got close to the house, my mother would come running up, I could hear her little footsteps and already the words she uttered to sympathize and congratulate me. My poor Raj, my little Raj, my big boy, well done.

Once she had relieved me of that load my body shook and I collapsed on the ground like a puppet. I saw little dark spots in front of my eyes. My mother prepared a large glass of water with plenty of sugar in it and I would drink it with many a click of my tongue and a "hmmm" which arose from deep in my throat. Afterwards I remained stretched out on the grass and my muscles were so heavy and painful that I often felt as if the earth were swallowing me up.

An hour later I would go to hand over my father's lunch, and once more made the same detour to return to my hiding-place. Each midday I hoped, more and more strongly as the days went by, to see the boy with the golden hair again. To that god of the evenings, whom I asked for peaceful nights, I prayed that he would bring David back to me. But for two good weeks, perhaps longer, I did not see him again. The others were there, the bell, the way they shuffled their feet and lingered unmoving in corners where there was shade, other thin children appeared, but not the one I was looking for, who had wept and whom I had kept company with in his sadness.

From my bush I also observed my father and he did not frighten me. My father opened and closed the prison gate, he had a set of keys deep in his pocket which made a bulge at the top of his thigh. When my father ran you could hear him from a long way off, he rattled and did not frighten me.

My father saluted a lot, often trotting along after cars, and bringing cups of tea on a tray to his bosses, I think that was all his job was. On Friday he cut flowers and handed them to the governor's driver, who wrapped them in newspaper. Neither spoke and they did it all fast, for fear of their hands touching, then my father went back to his quarters and the driver stationed himself under the mango tree, where he would wait, sitting on one of the stools. He was waiting for the prison governor, an Englishman called Mr Singer whom I saw from time to time. He was a very smartly dressed man, whose clothes were as new as those my mother starched and ironed. When Mr Singer arrived, the policemen stood to attention. My father, for his part, made a kind of ridiculous low bow and remained bent double like that until the governor was inside the house with the mauve flowers.

Occasionally when all was quiet, my father came and smoked a cigarette under the canopy, beside the bougainvilleas, and I would stare hard at him. At home he would quickly have shouted out why are you staring like that, what's your problem? But here, no, he was a little fellow with a drab uniform, his shirt outside his trousers – not like the policemen with their shirts tucked in and belts – and here, at such moments, he did not frighten me.

As he carried the tray with two cups, a teapot and biscuits, taking little steps, his trouser bottoms would get caught up with his sandals, but on he went, just the same, his eyes fixed on the tray, little steps, little steps, I wanted to fling stones at him, I wanted him to stumble, I wanted him to lose his temper and turn into the man I knew, who would not have let the bottoms of his trousers get caught under his sandals, who would have taken long strides, as if to give him a better run up, fling his arm up high in the air and hammer it down beside me, upon me, upon my mother.

One morning Madame Ghislaine told me it was Christmas. She had already folded up the sheet, but instead of returning post haste to her sewing machine she said to me in a hoarse voice:

"What a good boy you are. I know it's Christmas, but what can you do? That's how it is. When you have to work, you have to work. No?"

It was the first time I had heard that word and although for several weeks I had only opened my mouth to say, as my mother had taught me, *Bonjour Madame. Merci Madame. A demain, Madame,* I asked: "What's Christmas?"

She was knotting the sheet at that moment, but her hands stopped moving, she looked into my eyes and covered her mouth with her right hand, as if to stifle a cry. And then, I can remember as if it were yesterday, her eyes quite suddenly filled with tears, as if she had held them back all her life and now, faced with my question, it was too much for her and everything was unleashed at once. She lifted me up by the armpits as easily as a common or garden pot of flowers and set me down on an armchair. There she began telling me about Jesus, the little boy born in a stable and his magnificent, perfect mother, about the star which led the kings to him, about the good, kind man he became, this Jesus, the miracles he performed, about this son of God who loved everyone and wept with the poor, about this handsome and good God who ended on the cross and who forgave. Christmas, she said, was the day of this God's birth 1,944 years ago. Sometimes she said God, sometimes she said the son of God, sometimes the good Jesus, but what stuck in my memory was that this Jesus performed miracles, he had walked on the water! The dressmaker with her red and white house clasped my hands and spoke warmly to me, as sometimes my teacher did at school, and told me that on this holy day which was called Christmas, children could ask baby Jesus (or the son of God or the good Jesus) for whatever they wanted and there would be a miracle.

That day on the long road home, weighed down by that sheet, I did not suffer as I usually did. I was thinking about this God who walked on the water and I thought about our stream that had turned into a torrent of mud and I thought that if our family prayed to Him, as Madame Ghislaine had told me, if we changed gods, as Madame Ghislaine had advised me, perhaps if I asked for that magnificent, marvellous thing – to see my two brothers again – if I dared to have this wish, then the miracle might . . . Along the way this incredible idea, this mad hope grew and swelled within me, giving me a blazing energy, and I carried the bundle as if my brothers were there, Anil in front, Vinod just behind, each of them with a bundle, too, the way we used to carry buckets in the old days, and the three of us were confronting life together once more.

When my father came home, I told him about Jesus, the God who walked on the water and performed miracles. I was so excited by this news that I had not paid attention to his staggering gait, I failed to smell the alcohol, I observed neither his reddened eyes nor his swollen mouth. By the time I noticed all this, all that my mother had taught me to see, to interpret, the signs that heralded a night when we should be as silent as possible, invisible, immobile, by the time I noticed all this, it was already too late.

My father had the suppleness of a feline, a way of pouncing upon us, as if we were the prey he had tracked and cornered. He always dealt with my mother first and as he advanced on her she backed away, her hands held in front of her, spread out, her poor wrinkled hands, an absurd protection, a laughable defence. Am I now inventing the smile on my father's face? Am I inventing his eyes, suddenly so alive, so cruel? And if I say that he took pleasure in acting thus, is it my old man's voice or my little boy's memory dictating this to me?

In a single movement, just one, my father seized my mother's hands and twisted them until she cried out. Then he struck, one hand clamped round those of his wife, the other raised high above his head, behind his shoulder, what incredible strength my father had at moments like this, what strength he had, this man – whom I resembled during my youth, fortunately, heaven help us, only physically, but even this I regretted every time I caught sight of my reflection in a mirror – where did it come from, this strength, why did he use it like this? He was drunk, but he struck with precision and patience. He landed a clout, hard and flat, and my mother's head swung to one side. He waited until she was looking at him again before landing another blow, just as hard, just as precise, and went on until my mother's head was bowed. My father shook her like a rag doll and flung her to the ground and while waiting for this moment, I, little Raj, was praying to God that He would do something, now, at once, something that would turn this man to stone, that would make him fall forwards, slide into sleep, I do not know, I no longer know, what I was asking of this God, but I was praying hard that something should happen before my father's blows killed my mother and killed me too.

I was waiting for him to finish with her, waiting for him to start on me, I was waiting for the one moment when I could help my mother. Oh, how many times did I attempt to separate them, how many times did I leap onto my father, but, as I have already said, he was a big cat, we were his prey and that was a battle in which I never won. So when he flung my mother aside I caught her as she fell. That was all I did, all I could do. I had seen Anil doing this at Mapou. Catching her so that her head did not shatter on the hard floor of that house in the forest. But hardly had I felt my mother's weight when my father's hand was already beside me, upon me, smashing my mouth, whistling past my ear, closing my eyes, breaking open my nose. My father did not utter a word, he even seemed to have stopped breathing. My mother was weeping and trying to stand up, pleading, and, as for me, all I could hear was the roar of a torrent of mud. It was my first Christmas.

The days after my father's fits of madness were all alike. My mother and I would remain at home, dazed, stunned, our actions lethargic, feeling weak in the head. My mother would spend hours concocting poultices, infusions, potions and lotions from herbs, roots, leaves and flowers which she gathered in the forest and she would heal our wounds. But on this day of 26 December, 1944, her medicine was not enough. I do not know what really happened that morning, perhaps I failed to wake up, perhaps my mother's concoctions had no effect. I remember my father speaking in a voice that was quite unfamiliar to me, a little voice, almost a woman's voice, explaining to someone or other that I had fallen out of a tree and that I was unruly, then they put me in prison, along with the bAd mEn, the rObbers and the rUnaways. I guessed this when, borne in my father's arms, I passed under the great mango tree and heard the swish of his trouser bottoms as they got caught under his clattering sandals.

He stopped several times and each time in his womanish voice he said, in French, fell out of the tree. I did not know my father spoke French, enough, at least, to lie and cover up what he had inflicted on his own son. Indeed, maybe he spoke English or Spanish or Chinese as well, nothing would have surprised me, the truth was I did not know him at all. Between us lay the insurmountable wall of violence and death. I was thinking about my mother and when he put me down in a bed I cried myself to sleep. I had never slept in a bed before. At Mapou and in our forest house we used to sleep on mats made of dried palm leaves. I can recall how at one moment, there on the bed in this hospital at the heart of the prison – yes, there was a hospital there and at the time it did not strike me as strange, I knew no other prisons and so for me every prison had a mango tree, a gate with a pictorial sign on it, flowers and a lawn, huts, shade, smartly dressed policemen, sad ghosts and, why not? a hospital – so, there on the bed, for the first time in months I thought about the great clouds of white steam that used to float above the cane fields, near the camp at Mapou and how I used to wish I could spend my life inside them.

I think I slept a lot. I was not in very good shape: a broken nose, cracked ribs, bruises, a blue pulp instead of a mouth. When I think back to all this, it is my son that comes to mind and I picture him again at the age of eight trying out his first bike. His concentration was intense: pedalling, gripping the handlebars with both hands, maintaining his balance, watching the road and keeping an eye on me, behind him, for, like all fathers, had I not promised not to let go of him? I remember his look, shining with joy and the grin from ear to ear which had remained on his face from the moment he received his present that morning. He began pedalling quite fast, I could hear my wife and my mother behind me, laughing and encouraging my son and, as he was managing well without me, I let go of him. A few yards further on my son looked back and the shocked glance he threw behind him and the child's cry, alarmed at suddenly being on his own and, although I knew I had been right to let him pedal on his own, for that is how you learn to ride a bike, I remember the feeling of guilt that gripped me . . .

If I picture him for one second in the state I was in on that 26 December 1944, before I had reached the age of nine, I want to howl.

I slept a lot and when I opened my eyes there were ghosts with coloured eyes and pale skin around my bed and I had already seen these ghosts before, wandering about in a sun-drenched compound where a great mango tree stood. I felt as if I were in a world of cotton wool, muffled sounds, subdued light, my body engulfed by the mattress and the white sheet.

Several times a face crowned with filaments of gold would come and softly touch my face, where it was all swollen and blue. If I opened my eyes when he was above my head, he smiled, he had recognized me as the boy in the bush. He had only seen me for a few minutes, but I was convinced, and I still am, that he recognized me as soon as he saw me, identified me physically, but also recognized my unhappiness and I felt very calm, as if I were in one of my hiding-places, and here no-one could take my brothers away from me or do me harm.

6

I WAS WOKEN BY ONE OF THE PATIENTS SHOUTING. It was afternoon, I could tell this from the dull yellow light and the heavy heat swirling all around me. It was an old woman, the oldest I had ever seen, although there were certainly some old people at Mapou! This one was sunk deep in her bedclothes and from a distance you might have thought it was an empty bed, had it not been for her raising her rickety arm from time to time. When the nurses arrived she sprang up. I was observing all this from behind my mosquito net, six beds away from there – I had counted – and even I gave a start. She had a face as if crushed by something, flattened and all wrinkled. The skin around her eyes had been sucked inwards, which gave the impression that her eye sockets might topple into her head from one moment to the next. The old woman grabbed hold of one of the nurses by the neck and everyone, myself included, cried out. Strangely enough, I did not immediately realize that they were speaking in a language that was unknown to me. A doctor arrived and it took three adults to cope with the old lady. They tied her to the bed with sheets and these three big, strong adults ended up leaning against the end of the iron bed panting, as if they had been running all round the forest.

A nurse saw me sitting up, propped up on my elbows, and came over to me. She looked at me with her blue eyes and this made a great impression on me. She placed her hand on my brow, took out a thermometer from one of her pockets, thrust it under my tongue for a moment and said, in French: "Your fever's gone. You'll be able to go home soon."

She lingered at the foot of my bed with her hands in her pockets for a while, as if she wanted to say something to me, then she rearranged the mosquito net around my bed and went away. As she made her way through the ward, arms were raised in the beds, pleading and begging. She walked slowly, her head bowed, alone in the world. When she reached the end she turned and made a broad, slow gesture with her hand, sweeping across the ward, and all the arms were lowered. I told myself that perhaps in their language it was a way of calling for calm, of saying, just a little more patience.

I was thinking about all this when David came up to my bed. I heard him, of course, with the noise he made, walking a little awkwardly, thumping upon the ground at every step, it was as if he had lumps of iron in his feet.

How can I explain what I felt when he came and stood in front of me, with his fair hair, his green eyes, his hollow cheeks, that little smile of his – the trick he had of turning up just one corner of his mouth, people these days might call it a mocking smile, but it was not that at all, it was a long way from irony, something David was quite simply not capable of, no, it was like the preliminary sketch for a smile, the start of something better, something beautiful, which would give one pause, eagerly awaiting what came next – his shirt was old like mine, a part of the gold chain that hung about his neck fell into the hollow of his collar-bone, climbing up the protruding bone again before disappearing beneath the grey fabric, he had a tentative way of pushing aside the mosquito net and looking at me with the same benevolence as that first time, the time we had wept together . . . I was so happy to see him again and, above all, so reassured that he really existed!

To begin with he said things to me very softly in that strange, breathy language. This did not alarm me and his murmuring continued for quite a while. He was leaning over towards me and his speech was a long shushing sound that calmed me greatly, as if a prayer had been whispered in my ear. And indeed, perhaps it was a prayer. I regret not understanding what he was saying to me, what was in his heart that he wanted to share with me, even before we had told one another our names, but I listened to him, watching him attentively, and felt at ease, enveloped by his presence and his words. When he had finished he stood up and stared at me. I had the impression he was waiting for me to speak and so I said, speaking in French, as I had learned to at school, separating out the syllables, with a picture in my head of this sentence being written out by an imaginary hand as I spoke it, "My name is Raj and I live in Beau-Bassin."

David looked at me and said to me, just as slowly: "My name is David and I live here. But I used to live in Prague."

I did not doubt for a second that Prague was located here, in our country, somewhere a little hidden away, a little forgotten, as Mapou was. I remember there being a map of our island on the wall at school, but Mapou was not on it and I had pointed this out to Mademoiselle Elsa. She showed me Pamplemousses, and another town whose name I cannot recall, and she said it was round about there, twirling her fingers, smiling at me, and explaining that she was very sorry but only the most important cities and large towns were shown on a map. That afternoon when David told me he had lived in Prague earlier, I naturally assumed it must be somewhere hereabouts, lost between two important towns, a simple village, too insignificant to be shown on a map.

"Why are you in prison?"

"I don't know. Why are you?"

"I don't know."

"Are you Jewish?"

"No."

"Is your *maman* here?"

"No, she's at home. Is yours?"

"She's dead. My father's dead, too. Have you got any brothers and sisters?"

"No, I'm all alone."

"Me too."

I think that is how it went. After all these years I scratch around and delve into my memory and allowances must be made for me as it is sometimes more difficult than I expected. It may well be that was not the order in which he told me things, it is very likely my mind has rearranged my memories a little, but what I am absolutely sure of is that we talked very slowly for hours, in the fading light of the afternoon. The French words we used were foreign to both of us, from now on it was a language we had to bend to what was in our own minds, to what we wanted to say, no longer, as at school, simply decoding and repeating. We were both making the same effort to communicate and we were doing it slowly, patiently, which may be the reason why we were very quickly able to say important things to one another, such as I'm all alone. Me too.

That evening the nurse with blue eyes wished us a Happy New Year. She spread her hands wide and clapped them together several times. It was a kind of slow-motion applause and it was very odd. No-one responded. I had my face to the wall, I was thinking of my mother, I hoped she was waiting for me at home and I told myself I was nine. My mother had told me that on the first of January I should be a year older. Soon I would be as old as Anil. I thought about the clothes we had been given at Mapou, those clothes that made us look so special and in which my brothers had died.

In the night David came and woke me up. I was only half asleep, like the majority of the patients in the ward and I was learning that illness is not a silent thing. I followed him in the darkness, his pale shirt acting as a beacon, this reminded me of Anil and the day of the deluge but I continued following him, softly, step by step. David's way of walking made me laugh, he knew he was noisy and he wanted to get better at it but in vain. He seemed to be the most ethereal boy on earth, full of grace and indeed it all started well: he would lift his knee, raise it high and slowly, very slowly, advance his leg in front of him, but instead of placing his foot softly on the ground he abruptly let it go, as if he were suddenly tired and could no longer control his movements. At each clump! he froze and, in the darkness I imagined his fair hair shivering, but no-one paid us any attention, not even the duty nurse who, unless she were deaf, must surely have heard us. Since David had been in the hospital I think he had been going out like this every night, it was the only way he could be a child and the patients in this dirty ward, stifling and crammed with groaning and lamentation, had all understood this and let him wander at will.

I still had painful ribs, a swollen nose, lips enclosed in a fragile crust that threatened at every moment to crack into a trickle of blood. David had bouts of fever brought on by malaria and spent half his time emptying himself into the latrines or his bed, and was receiving serum treatment, but all that became trivial on account of the excitement we felt that night, slipping outside, like real rObbers.

The hospital was tucked away at the heart of the prison, at the northern end, a part I had not been able to see from my hiding-place. At the centre of the prison there was another wall that separated the men's quarters from the women's, and the hospital was in the area reserved for women. David explained all this to me in our night-time games.

David needed no light when we crept out of the hospital, he knew everywhere by heart. For three nights we did exactly the same thing, as children do all over the world, we established a routine, a ritual. We would wait for the end of supper, the curfew, and those lamentations which the night summons up in the sick and sorrowful, and then, at last, we had hours without disruption, a half-light we could rely on like a faithful friend who doesn't let you down. I would follow him, I would listen, and for a few hours I would forget Mapou, my mother, my brothers, my father and not once did the vastness of the night frighten me or make me want to dig a hole and bury myself in it. We could convince ourselves that what we had was one great playground. During the daytime it was impossible to believe this, the walls were dark, there was barbed wire everywhere you looked, a policeman with his truncheon in every corner, the sun acting as a searchlight, no hiding-place to take shelter in, no games to play. And in any case I myself was not allowed to leave the hospital ward.

Games were our fraternal language. Listening to our footsteps suddenly muffled by the grass which heralded the dividing wall, following his mop of hair, not letting that blond halo out of my sight for a second, focusing all my strength on this goal, not losing him, listening to the approach of the wind that caused the dry leaves to rustle in the eucalyptus to our left near the women's section, using our handkerchiefs to catch the insects fluttering round the oil lamps near the hospital, laughing when we heard the policeman on duty humming a song, as he went hmm, hmm, hmm, very shrilly, and collapsing with laughter without uttering a single sound, just letting our bodies shake with merriment and giving ourselves a pain in the stomach. Teaching him how to put your foot down soundlessly, to keep your arms to your sides so as to slip more easily between two trees, to walk along an imaginary line without ever deviating – to close your eyes and imagine we were crossing a bridge over a river in spate – and, for the first time, to play at aeroplanes.

David climbed on top of me and lay flat along my arms, his body stiff, his arms stretched out, ready to fly. He was a year older than me but, for once, I was the stronger. Holding his feather weight, his no-weight-at-all, in my arms, I spun round and round and round in the darkness. We felt the wind beating against our faces, as the half-light became a black whirlwind and it took all our willpower to contain the rare exhilaration we felt in our stomachs, and not to shout for joy. When we slipped back into our beds I experienced such excitement and such pride at not having been caught that I found it hard to still my beating heart, telling myself how good we were at this game. Clearly we were just children, believing ourselves to be free because it was dark and we could not see the wall or the barbed wire. Today I am convinced that the nurses, the patients, the doctors and even the policeman on duty knew that David and I played outside after nightfall, but those adults also knew that, as there was no way out, at all events we could not go very far.

During the day I remained in bed and slept a good deal. I dreamed of my brothers, of my mother, I dreamed of school and remained as discreet and silent as possible. What I wanted was for them to forget me, for the night to come quickly so I could meet David again. There were a great many comings and goings, many tears, even on the part of the nurses. Sometimes there was anger, too, the patients hurled their trays against the walls, spitting and yelling, filled with hatred, I suppose, for this prison, this island.

All the patients used to talk about a ship coming, it was their constant obsession. When the doctor made his morning visit, whenever a policeman passed through on his rounds, they were forever asking when the ship would be sailing back to Eretz. During my stay at the hospital I had come to realize that they were not people from our island and this had seemed very strange to me. Was that why they had been locked up? I asked myself.

One morning I sensed a change in the atmosphere of the dormitory even before I opened my eyes. Generally it was very quiet in the morning, it seemed as if the patients found it hard to wake up, as if it took them time to realize where they really were, perhaps during the night they dreamed of their land, their Eretz, and when it grew light they clung to their dreams, which was what gave this strange mood of hope to the dormitory at dawn. On this particular day, on the contrary, I sensed a commotion and when I opened my eyes the patients were almost all sitting up in their beds and everywhere there was whispering. When I caught the eyes of some of them they smiled at me and, for the first time, some of them even gave me a little wave. The nurses were gathered together and chatting cheerfully. Then a policeman came in and announced loud and clear that, despite the rumour, there would not be a ship for Haifa that evening and the war was not yet over. I never forgot that sentence. It made no sense to me at the time and yet I guessed that what it signified was terrible. There were no exclamations, no protests, as if it were not the first time their hopes had been dashed. The patients lay down again, the nurses went out and it was a sad, grey dormitory once more.

David had told me his parents were dead. When we talked we did it with lots of gestures and mimicry, a little like deaf people. When he was telling me this he had closed his eyes and tilted his head suddenly on one side, to make it clear to me that they were dead. They were all on their way to Eretz. Is it far to Eretz? he had asked me. I had no idea but I promised to ask my teacher at school, who knew everything.

I told him I, too, had been on a journey before coming here, because that was how I saw things at that age, kilometres and oceans made no difference, both David and I had left the places where we were born and had each followed our parents to a strange, mysterious and somewhat frightening spot, where we hoped to escape from adversity.

I do not know if I ought to be ashamed to say this, but that was how it was: I did not know there was a world war on which had lasted for four years and when David asked me at the hospital if I was Jewish I did not know what it meant, I said no, being under the vague impression that, because I was in hospital, being Jewish referred to an illness. I had never heard of Germany, in reality I knew very little. In David I had found an unhoped for friend, a gift from heaven, and at the start of this year of 1945 that was all that counted for me.

To tell him my brothers were dead I had imitated him, I closed my eyes and tilted my head on one side. But then, of course, there came this knot tightening within me, mounting higher, higher, higher. We were sitting behind the hospital beneath the canopy and five steps away from us there was the outer wall. A fine, heavy rain was falling and it was my last night there but I did not yet know this. David, orphaned, exiled, deported, suffering from malaria and dysentery, comforted me. He brought his head close to mine and even today I still seem to feel his soft curls on the right side of my face. I have certainly forgotten many things from those days spent at the hospital, but his golden curls and their silken touch belong to me for all eternity.

The nurse with blue eyes woke me that morning. She gathered up the mosquito net and fastened it all into one large knot. Even before she spoke a word or made a gesture to indicate that I should get out of bed, I knew. I had no choice but to follow her. David was sitting on his bed and he stared at me without moving. I gave him a little wave but he did not respond. That was hurtful to me, for it was as if he did not know me, as if he were looking through me, had already forgotten me. I walked slowly, my head bowed, with heavy steps, all the weight of my body concentrated in the soles of my feet. Suddenly, behind me, a clattering sound. I looked back. David was walking like a crab, a little bit to the left, a little bit to the right, and making signs with his hands to tell me to wait. I stopped and smiled, I was happy, I had been mistaken, of course he knew me, he had been caught unawares, just now, not knowing what to do, that was why his eyes were blank. My heart turned over, from dejection to joy, like the flip of a coin, my entire body straightened up, as if by magic, my feet were no longer leaden and I was poised to spring towards him, to play at aeroplanes, to leap about, play and tell stories.

But that is not what happened. The nurse picked me up like a parcel and swung me into the hard, hairy arms of a policeman. I heard David calling me, then shouting out things in his language, but I did not struggle, I did not yell, I was quite simply incapable of it. A great stone was falling within me and crushing everything, my throat, my heart, my stomach, my belly. We moved from a square of sunlight to a square of shadow and the policeman held me out to my father. They said things which I cannot remember. My father put me down onto the ground and kept his hand on the back of my neck. His hand was hot and clammy. At a distance it could have seemed like a gesture of affection, but it was not. He was keeping me on a leash, that is the truth, ready to shake me by the scruff of the neck like a dog. At one moment he laughed and covered his mouth with his fingers. He never did that at home.

The gate opened, my father pushed me out and in no time at all I was in my mother's arms. She held me clasped to her all the way and she ran, my poor mother, in a hurry to get away from that prison. My head was leaning against her shoulder and I saw the walls disappearing behind the trees. My mother was weeping and talking at the same time. She often did that. She told me what she had done in my absence, every morning she had stood in front of the prison gate, hoping to see me, every evening she had begged the policeman on duty to give me the pot of milk she had bought, but he had never yielded. She had gone down on her knees to my father, for him to bring me home, but he had not yielded either. Previously my mother's love would have swamped me with emotion, but now, as we advanced deeper into the forest, I had only one thing on my mind: finding David again.

7

My mother was convinced that the hospital did not really know how to cure people. Every evening she applied a yellow cream with a rancid taste to my still sensitive lips and gently massaged my sides with a thick oil. She placed her outspread hands at the base of my ribs, it was like an angel's wings being laid on my stomach, she would close her eyes and if I remained still I could feel the blood pulsing in her veins. Her hands had something mysterious about them. She knew how to find herbs and leaves, she knew their language: touched by her fingers, every plant found its destined purpose: healing, protecting, soothing, sometimes killing. At Mapou people would come to her with a pain or a wound and in a whisper she would give them the name of a plant with some instructions, then, if it worked, a few days later we would find a fruit, a vegetable, a handful of rice or some sugar outside our door.

My mother never spoke to me about plants, but I know she passed on a little of her knowledge to my son. It has always amused me to see him, someone whose work is in a world of technology, meticulously tending his garden and among the bookcases filled with science-fiction novels and computer manuals at his house there is a shelf devoted to herbal medicine and botany. When I spend the weekend with him at his home, where one can hear the gushing stream lower down the hillside, I know my mother lives on in him a little: I see him opening and closing his jars of dried herbs, I watch him weighing out and mixing together unknown roots, purchased at great expense, and when he prepares a delicious infusion for us to drink on the terrace in the evening, and I compliment him on the drink he does not reply that it is one of my mother's recipes, instead he says to me in a disarming way: this is *grandmère*.

After my return home at the start of 1945 few things had changed outwardly. The forest surrounded us, sometimes it felt to me like a belt drawn so tight that it was suffocating my family, sometimes it protected me like a shield. My father would come home in the evening and we kept as far away from him as possible. There was no doubt that one day he would start hammering his hand down again upon my mother, upon myself, it was simply a matter of time.

But since my return from the hospital I was no longer afraid, or more precisely, I now knew that there was something more to life than my father's rage. Following our arrival at Beau-Bassin a great part of my existence and my energy had revolved around that violence. Now I knew there were other things that mattered more.

After school I would run without stopping until the rush of air into my mouth grated on my parched throat. I would return to my hiding-place in front of the prison barbed wire and wait for David. During the three weeks following my release he did not appear. Other prisoners, yes. Always at the same time of day when the sun was in their eyes, its rays slanting at an angle, soon to disappear behind the hill where I lurked. I would remain there until the second bell rang, the one that sent them back to their living quarters. Occasionally I would recognize one of the patients from the hospital, which made me glad, and, naïve child that I was, I would wave my hand, knowing they could not see me but, how can I put it? I followed the dictates of my heart.

I was too little to understand what was unfolding in front of my eyes, but the mixture of nervousness and curiosity that had initially drawn me there, hoping to see rObbers, bAd mEn and rUnaways, had disappeared. Now that I knew who was hidden there within the darkness of the pathways, knew the walls that towered around them, had heard the sound of the grass beneath their feet, heard their singing in the evening, I viewed them with great sadness and went on waiting for my friend. If David did not come out to exercise it was because he was still in the hospital.

During those long weeks I did not abandon hope. I persisted seriously, methodically. When I came home from the prison I would be sweating, my clothes covered in twigs, leaves and mud. My mother would be waiting for me in silence, she never asked me for an explanation of these escapades after school. I had returned safe and sound, I was back before my father, that was what mattered to her. She took my clothes, aired them, beat them with a kind of flat wooden spoon and in the morning I would find them almost clean; in those days I wore the same clothes for a week at a time. In the evening, after supper, I used to stay out of doors, watching nature as much as it seemed to be watching me. We very rarely notice changes within ourselves at the time, we perceive them later, in the light of events and our reactions to them, but, sitting there as I did, motionless in the dark, I sensed it, a change in myself, I felt as if I were getting bigger, growing, like the trees around me, and it seemed to me that the exhalation of the green, dark forest had something to do with it. I was still puny, my clothes fluttered loosely about me, my mother could still close her hand around my calf, but there was this new hope within me, the promise of a less lonely life, the bond that had formed between David and myself.

I am sure that if I had had to wait countless weeks before seeing David again it would not have been a problem for me. I was one of those children who learn early in life that nothing comes easily, quickly and without effort. When I went to ground in my hiding-places and my feet grew numb I did not get up, I did not shake myself, I stayed put, motionless, and only that way could I forget everything.

So this is what my life came down to for many days in a row: waiting for the end of lessons, slipping out of the classroom, running strenuously, without flagging. Stones, thickets, branches, earth, the darkness of the forest, all these were nothing to me compared with my goal. Sometimes, as I slithered in under the bushes, alongside the barbed-wire fence, my body flat upon the leaves, I would have a blackout, my body suddenly heavy. But I was prepared for this. In a screw of paper I kept a few spoonfuls of cocoa, which I used to filch during the break at school. I also kept the dried fruit from the afternoon snack which the school gave us, and with all this I calmed my shaking and the little black spots gathering before my eyes gradually vanished. I stayed there until the last of the prisoners disappeared and my father left his post beside the gate and went back into the shade of the mango tree, until the policemen returned inside the house with the bougainvilleas and the picture became unmoving, neat and tidy once more. Then I went home, hardly disappointed, hardly at all. But with the emptiness there was in my little life, as a boy with no brothers, no toys, no laughter, no freedom from care, I was all the more determined to see David again and I would wait for the next day.

Several times during this period, my father advanced on us with great strides, flinging out his hands and feet and all that I have related before began again, like a stage play he performed to perfection. Since my stay in the hospital, however, my father now had a new weapon: a bamboo cane that could inflict pain, lacerate and burn, but could not crack ribs, break arms and noses, or split open lips. This new cane, thicker and greener than before, reminded me of Mapou and the one, all ribs and knots, with a fine tip, which he had left behind in our house made of cowpats and straw, and, curiously enough, I found this memory comforting. I can picture myself going up to it, feeling the weight of it, peering inside it, into the stem, disappointed not to see light at the other end, and putting it back in its place against the wall with a feeling of nostalgia coming over me. Perhaps because back there at Mapou there were more of us, I had two brothers to protect me and my father had friends and his pride, perhaps back there he was not quite so bad . . .On days after the nights when he beat us I would stay at home, incapable of moving, my limbs throbbing with pain, the shouting still present in my head. My mother would vanish into the forest and return an hour later, carrying in her hands the herbs, roots and leaves she had picked. On such days the battle was won by my father, his rage and his violence, once more he occupied all the space in my life and all my new-found strength and proud resolution ebbed away.

Several weeks had passed. As I have said, I was not counting the days, I was not impatient, I had not given myself a date beyond which I would no longer go to the prison. At the start of 1945 it was very hot. All around our house the grass had dried and turned brown. Our well was drying up more and more and we had to lower the bucket down deeply to draw water. In the morning you could already feel the shimmering of the heat all around. At night the insects flitted about for a long time, maddened by the temperature, and if you cocked an ear the burnt grass sometimes crackled under the footfall of a rodent, a feral cat, a stray dog. The forest had lost some of its green brilliance and its density, it seemed to be drawing back from our house, exposing us more and more to the immensity of the sky and the sun's fiery swords.

On the day when I finally saw David again the spry, colourful flowers, the thick, green lawn, the mango tree with its shade and dense foliage, the hungry, fast-growing bougainvilleas, all were as if stricken by a blistering flash of lightning and the result was a prospect now much reduced, shrivelled, petrified. My own bush was no longer the same and I had to resort to dry branches, twigs and leaves to camouflage myself. The bell rang and, as always, my heart began to beat a little faster. David was the first to appear and this gave me a shock, I had always come prepared to search for him, to track him down, as it were. The others appeared slowly and then for the most part did not stir. David walked the length of the house with the bougainvilleas, he leaned against its wooden wall and stared towards me. A few feet away from him a policeman kept removing his cap to mop his head with a handkerchief. I emerged from my hiding-place, and crawled right up to the barbed wire, staying as close to the ground as possible. David was looking towards the place where he had sat down and wept, where he had smiled at me with that smile of his, that way he had of turning up one side of his mouth, which I had often sought to imitate though with no other result than a twisted grimace. Watch, crawl, wait, pray. I prayed that the policeman would go away, so that I could stand up, make a signal, wave my shirt, my canvas bag, tell him I'm here, I've always been here, won't leave you in this prison, heavens above, just a few seconds, that was all I needed.

But the policeman remained close to David, they even exchanged a few words and the second bell rang out. David stepped away from the wall and moved into the shadows, followed by all the others. I was nine years old and the patience I had shown during those long weeks suddenly vanished. I held myself back from giving voice to the immense vexation I felt, I struck the ground with both my fists and grabbed hold of the barbed wire in a rage I had hitherto rarely known. My eyes were flooded with tears and the prison was no longer more than a blurred picture. Clenching my teeth, I plunged the palms of my hands into the metal coils, pain mingling with my anger, I shook the barrier with all my strength and with a dull sound something was suddenly uprooted like a rotten plant. A part of the barbed-wire fence came out of the ground. It vibrated.

If I had been struck by lightning it would have been no different. Everything stopped in me, the rage blinding me, the fury in my hands and feet, the flowing tears. I had become a dried-out bamboo. I slipped into my hiding-place. I waited, with fear in the pit of my stomach, but nobody came. I got up and walked home. Today, just as I remember David's golden curls, I can also remember the smell of rust and blood on my hands. In the forest on the way home I would sniff at my palms, as if they were a drug, and at each intake of breath I was infused with a surge of serenity and hope.

8

IT WAS THE CYCLONE WHICH STRUCK THE country that very evening that seems to have helped me most in this whole affair. When I got home that afternoon, with the smell of rust and blood on my hands, the sun was a pale yellow disk behind dense, dark clouds, and, veiled as it was, we could gaze at it. My mother was peering at the sky the way she once used to peer at the cumulus clouds clinging to the mountain at Mapou, her hands on her hips, sniffing the air. I went up to her and, without looking down, she held out an arm and drew me to her and we remained like this for a moment. I still remember it, nature and my mother seemed to be on the alert, while I, little Raj, I felt, yes, I think I can say this, I felt good. Just there, at this very moment, with my head buried in her waist, feeling her hand on my shoulder, while I am hugging and squeezing her waist, at this moment I am thinking of David, I am thinking of the torn-up barbed wire, the warmth of my mother melts on my arms and I feel good. My mother was the tender side of our life of poverty, sadness and beatings from a bamboo cane. She loved me, she protected me, she healed me, she spoke softly to me, she was tender, fed me with her bare fingers when I was ill and her patience seemed limitless. I have never seen its like in anyone else and it was thanks to this patience, thanks to the way she had of seeing everything through to the end, even if it was painful and slow, I think it was to this that she owed the way she had with plants. My mother was the good fortune in my life, what existence gave me to stop me going off the rails, to keep me on the right road, a pillar of strength, of goodness, of constancy and self-sacrifice, helping me to grasp that there was something more to life, and with her at my side during my childhood, I became neither mad, wicked, nor despairing.

Like me, my mother carried the deaths of Anil and Vinod within her throughout her life, and, like me, she was never able to put this bereavement into words. You can say you are an orphan, or a widow or a widower, but when you have lost two sons on the same day, two beloved brothers on the same day, what are you? What word is there to say what you have become? Such a word would have helped us, we should have known precisely what we were suffering from when tears came inexplicably to our eyes and when, years later, all it took was a smell, a colour, a taste in the mouth, to plunge us into sadness once more, such a word could have described us, excused us and everyone would have understood.

After a long while, unmoving, my mother said to me, still looking at the sky: "No school tomorrow."

And it was the signal the forest, the clouds and the world around us had been waiting for. The wind got up, ran right through the forest, everything shook and around us the woods sang a long and beautiful lament. Low clouds, ragged and dark, like malevolent ghosts, sped rapidly by above us, while those clinging to the vault of heaven grew more dense, threatening. The crowns of the trees were dancing against this ballet of the clouds, a flock of birds took to the air at top speed, calling out, and behind us, all of a sudden, lightning flashed and, as Anil had taught me to do, I counted, to know how far away the thunder was. One, two, three, four . . . The earth shook and, as if I had received a blow to the head, I cannot say why it did this to me, but in an instant I had travelled back in time and began yelling. Vinod, Anil, Vinod, Anil!

The cyclone lasted four days and four nights. It was a novelty for us to be protected by walls, the water seeped in everywhere, but the house did not collapse. Outside the forest snapped, crashed, resisted and it was as if a howling pack surrounded our house, a living creature in a frenzy. My father remained at the prison, trapped by the storm, and I wonder whether he knew how much my mother and I wept during those days. We were not afraid of the storm, we were not afraid of the wind, nor the rain's rapid gunfire, nor the branches and stones crashing against our walls. We were weeping for my brothers. The instant the thunder let rip it had seemed to us as if a gigantic, evil hand were there to snatch Vinod and Anil away from us, as if the house at Beau-Bassin, the forest, the prison, the new school, the long months since that day at Mapou, as if all that had been wiped away at a stroke and our hearts and our grief were newly raw. It was for moments like this that there should be a word to tell what one becomes forever when one loses a brother, a son.

On the fifth day a clear sky and a light that burst through here and there in clouds of steam around the forest revealed the devastated landscape to us. The clearing was strewn with timber, leaves, branches, dead animals, scrap metal. The most exposed trees, at the edge, lay on the ground, uprooted or broken in two, shattered. The forest seemed huddled in unbelievable stillness . . .

It took my father several hours to get back to our house because all the paths had disappeared and I may say he looked pleased to see us. We set to work without delay. Everything the wind had brought down which we could not use we burned behind the house at the end of the day. In one corner we stored pieces of wood, branches, cloth, scraps of metal, at that time anything could come in handy. The next day we took outside the stools, the wardrobe, the sleeping mats and the kitchen utensils and put them in the open to dry. A strong smell of mildew lingered in our house and my mother lit tiny fires of camphor and eucalyptus twigs in each corner of the house. Out in the sunlight my mother's copper bowls and saucepans gleamed like jewels and I never grew tired of admiring them. That evening my father came home sober, no songs, no curses, but with a bag of food. We had nothing left to eat. He had brought in potatoes, aubergines, mangoes and a pumpkin. The mangoes were soft and their skins black. Every potato was dark and rotten at its core. The pumpkin was waterlogged, translucent and spotted with green mould and to palliate the bitterness of the aubergines, my mother fried them with chilli, that favourite ingredient of the poor, for it would hide a stale taste in all foods. It burned our tongues, but we preferred this to the bitterness.

A few days later I finally plunged into the forest. A terrifying silence reigned there. All my landmarks, my favourite spots, my hiding-places, my secrets had disappeared: the mango trees, the banyans, the eucalypts, the nests, the holes, the mounds, the anthills, the fork of a tree, a footpath, a spring, the roots on which I used to sit. Everything was mixed up with everything else, stems and roots jumbled together, patches of sky opened up where, before the cyclone, there used to be refreshing shade, sometimes the earth had caved in upon itself, the very image of us human beings, grovelling on our knees before the might of a catastrophe, thousands of worms teemed there, feeding off the disaster in the basin thus created.

I reached the other end of the forest with great difficulty. The circular path that surrounded the prison fortress of Beau-Bassin had disappeared beneath fallen trees and mud. I turned to the left and beat myself a path to the top of the hill where the wall ended and the line of barbed wire began. There was shouting in the prison compound.

My father and the policemen were pressed up against the entrance gate. The prisoners were gathered in the compound and, together, they looked less pale, less weak. They were shouting, waving their arms in the air and the closer they drew to the gate the more my father and his henchmen flattened themselves against it. On the other side of the fence the prison governor's black car glittered in the sun. The mango tree had been uprooted and now lay across the house with the bougainvilleas. Its roots were reminiscent of an immense flower and I could not get over seeing this giant, once a haven of deep shade, with its compact foliage and juicy fruits, thus struck down. The mango tree had smashed through the governor's office. The prison compound looked like the clearing around our house, strewn with debris, no sign of the delicate and colourful flowers. At last this Beau-Bassin prison, in which Jews turned away from Palestine were being kept locked up, looked like what it truly was: a monstrous thing.

I was so taken up with studying the scene of devastation and watching the rebellion that I had rather forgotten David. I assumed he was in the middle of the group who were shouting, how could it be otherwise? The door of the black car opened and the governor stepped out, upright and gloved in his starched clothes. He looked with disdain at the prisoners who were still shouting, then he spat. That astonished me, coming from a gentleman like this, it was a great expectoration of disgust, for which he first raised his head high. The shouts redoubled, fists were waved in the air, the crowd of prisoners drew closer and closer to the gate, indifferent to the truncheons which the few policemen were whirling about in front of them. I was beginning to feel anxious about what would happen and at that moment I felt a cold hand on my shoulder.

Even today, although it makes me laugh a little, I can recall the sudden fear, like an electric shock, that made me utter a cry and leap up. Crouched and hunched up as I had been, I was incapable of breaking into a run, even though everything within me was straining to get away. No, for the first time in my life I got my feet in a tangle, and I, the king of the lightning-swift departure, fell over backwards. And, as I lay there on the ground, my heart thumping fit to burst, what I saw behind me was a boy with fair hair. That wretched David in fits of laughter.

How can I describe David when he laughed like that? He threw back his shoulders, slapping his thighs with his hands, opened his mouth wide, his body rocking back and forth, closed his eyes, choking with merriment, and until then I had never seen anyone laugh like this, without restraint, laughing, in fact, with the whole of his body. I gave him a friendly shove, pretending to be cross, and there we were on that February afternoon in 1945, two ordinary boys simply teasing one another, indifferent to the seriousness of the situation.

David had taken advantage of the chaos after the cyclone. I can readily imagine how those prisoners, coming from Czechoslovakia, from Poland, accustomed to a natural world which gives some warning, to seasons like autumn and spring, must have thought that the end of the world was nigh. David told the story of his escape, making broad gestures. He had gone to the fence, looking for me. Nobody had seen him, the crowd demonstrating shielded him from the gaze of the policemen and my father. He had called my name – and I remember how it constricted my heart when he was acting this out for me, cupping his hands round his mouth, Raj, Raj, Raj, Raj, are you there? And at that moment the only answer was silence and the ravages of the storm. I smiled when he showed me the fence uprooted out of the ground, he was very happy to have discovered this, very surprised, as I had been several days earlier.

Today when I close my eyes and picture him, sitting beside me, with a tangle of branches, leaves and shadows all around us, telling me about his escape, I find it hard to believe that this thin, blond little boy was ten. I was a good head taller than him and I could carry him, for he was even slighter than me, and yet at school I was the skinniest in my class.

His legs were white, almost translucent and his skin trembled like that of an old person, threatening to tear at every movement.

In those days I had not the least idea of how much time David had spent there. He felt he had been there for a very long while but to me this had no meaning. We remained in that damp hiding-place watching the turbulence in the compound. David was fidgeting a good deal. I told myself I must show him how to remain still, climb trees, run soundlessly, slip between two tree-trunks, bury yourself in the earth, creep behind a door, and the very thought of all these things that now awaited us, all those crowded days with David, filled me with such joy that I had to force myself not to get up, take him with me and start my new life straightaway.

Suddenly we heard an engine, the slamming of car doors and dozens of policemen with truncheons in their hands made their appearance beside the black car. As if by magic the iron gate of the prison opened and what happened now for several minutes was an extremely ugly thing for two children to see. The police charged the prisoners. My father ended up on the ground and as he was crawling painfully towards the fallen mango tree, the prisoners, taken by surprise, dispersed as rapidly as possible. Some of them were running as fast as they could in all directions, towards their dormitory or towards us, but they were quickly caught by the policemen and if they did not immediately obey, if they failed to go and kneel before the front steps of the gutted house, they were hauled over there unceremoniously. Their feet dragged against the ground, their shoes came off, they struggled, but they lacked strength. I wish I had never witnessed such a thing. The police were yelling, the people shouting, weeping, and David began to sob as well, unrestrainedly, as just now he had laughed so uproariously. I put my arm round his shoulder for I did not know what else to do and it was as if the storm had returned, with its uproar and its urge to smash everything.

Suddenly a youth came towards us, he might have been fifteen or sixteen, he outran the two men who were chasing him. He flung himself against the barbed wire, I still remember his face filled with rage, he was not afraid, this young man, he was not afraid of anything, not even of fences, I remember his body slamming against the fence with a metallic sound, the cry he repressed and the commands given by the policemen just behind him. It all happened so quickly. David surged forward and in an instant I flung my arm across his shoulder and hurled myself onto him. I do not know if the young man saw us, nor do I know if he was preparing to scale the barbed wire, I do not know anything, I just remember this thing that got hold of me, the instinct that had made me yell for hours in the storm the day my brothers died and throw Anil's stick into the stream. This other Raj within me plummeted onto David and put a hand over his mouth, immobilizing him. Three feet away from us the policemen also stopped the young man in his tracks with truncheon blows to the kidneys and dragged him back to the gutted house. I did not look at David, no, I could not have borne his gaze, but I felt all his strength beneath me, thrusting and struggling, and as I held him on the ground I was weeping, weeping, begging his forgiveness. When I think back to that I reassure myself as best I can, I tell myself that if I had not done that the policemen would have discovered David, would have brought him in, would have searched the forest, reinforced the fence. They would have discovered me, too, and who knows what would have been in store for me, at the prison and later, at the hands of my father? And I should have been alone again.

I am old now and can say it, with shame, with sorrow, hanging my head as low as possible. That was what I did at the age of nine: stopped David helping one of his comrades, a Jew like himself, locked up because no-one knew what to do with them, and if I had not acted in that way David might still be alive today.

9

I STILL WONDER WHY HE FOLLOWED ME. WHEN I let him go there were red marks around his mouth where my hands had muzzled him. I begged his forgiveness once more, I told him I had not wanted the policemen to see him, I implored his forgiveness again and again, but to no avail. There was no going back, no way I could undo what I had done.

The words collided with one another in my throat, came tumbling out of my mouth in a chaotic fashion, just as in a dream, when one is desperately trying to speak. I longed for him to understand my mother tongue so that what I was saying might flow more freely, so that I might use just the right word, express my precise feelings to him. Then I fell silent as he stared at me with dry, unmoving eyes, his face pale, his mouth streaked about with red and I was almost expecting him to hit me, already bracing my shoulders and fists to ward off the blows. David turned his head away and stared at the prison for a long time. Silent tears coursed down his cheeks in such a brutal manner that I was afraid this would never stop. For the first time since I had known him he was as unmoving as I myself had the habit of being and I think it was distress that made our bodies so rigid.

I did not know what to do, what to say, everything was colliding within me, my feelings and thoughts were in an unparalleled state of frenzy. And I was thinking about my brothers, about our stream and about Mapou, not about their deaths, for once, no, I was simply thinking about them, about their affectionate presence – I know that the man I have become owes them a great deal, for Anil and Vinod loved me in the simplest and most devoted manner possible, never letting our perpetual poverty embitter and warp our feelings. This takes a great deal of good nature and strength. I thought about the clouds of steam above the rippling green fields, about that syrupy aroma that arose from the cut canes at harvest time, when the pollen from the flowers hovered in the air. And I thought about my life since then, my mother, her courage and her outstretched hands facing my father and him, him, him, always him, smashing, breaking, preventing the making of anything at all. And David and the school and the prison and the forest and those grown-ups being dragged across the asphalt that ripped their skin and that young man throwing himself against the lacerating barbed wire and myself, so sad and so feeble, hurling myself at David and pinning him down, with a strength drawn from who knows where, gagging him by putting my fist between his teeth and enduring being bitten without flinching. And our new life at Beau-Bassin which appeared easier but was not, for it was enveloped in a great solitude now, without my brothers, without the neighbours, without the factory, without the stream and its faintly sugary water, without the cane fields and the factory chimney that used to belch forth those marvellous clouds.

There amid the bushes, beside an unmoving and furious David, the absurd and improbable idea came to me that I might perhaps have been happy back there, in the ramshackle hut at Mapou.

My heart was racing, I felt lost and on the brink of fainting. A weight pressed heavily on my stomach and a vague feeling overcame me, the precise nature of which I could not identify at the time. I believe that all I had lived through since the death of my brothers, every moment spent in that house in the depths of the forest, my afternoons focused on the prison, the upsurge of my father's violence, our life as a trio, the terrible scene I had just witnessed, all this, I believe, was distancing me from my childhood and even if that had not been brilliant, I still clung to it, in spite of everything. This feeling, like a rising and falling tide of nausea, was the loss of childhood and the awareness that nothing, nothing from now on, would protect me from the terrible world of men.

I had no idea what to do and yet I could not stay there. So I stood up and looked at David. The tears had traced two lines upon his face begrimed with mud and dust. He stood up as well and then and there, without a word, without a smile, without a look, he followed me.

He remained behind me and I was forever looking back to check that he was there. In the forest David drew closer to me, I think he was afraid, we were treading on branches, fallen tree-trunks and this was not very solid ground. We had hardly taken a few steps when David slipped on the damp branches and fell headlong. He looked at me dolefully, and when I helped him to his feet I said these words to him, precisely these, in this order: "Stay with me. Do what I do and we won't get separated. I promise you."

There is nothing remarkable about these words but I remember articulating them distinctly as I spoke them, just as if I were weighing each one of them, as if I were learning to say them for the first time, and yet I had not thought about it, this simple sentence had come to me naturally, for it was what my brothers would have said to me and what I would have said to my brothers if they had needed me.

The tension there had been between us, our faces frozen, his anger, my shame, all that melted quietly away in the battered forest. And during the days that followed, which we were to spend together, right up to the end, I did stay with him, I did protect him as best I could and I came close to fulfilling my promise completely, like a man of my word.

During that first journey through the forest I often held his hand. I showed him how to test the solidity of a branch on the ground. Put your foot on it, make it move to ensure that it doesn't roll, lean on it a little, don't stay standing on it for long, keep moving all the time and, above all, use your hands as much as possible to hold on to things and spread the weight of your body. I should say that it was not easy. David would slip, dragging me with him, and we often ended up in the mud. This forest we were in was new to him, just as it was to me, but I tried to put on a good front, to hold our course, steering by the details I had noted on the outward journey. I tried to remember what Anil did when we were going into an area for the first time and were relying on him for our safety, I tried to recall his face, his reassuring smile, his demeanour as the elder brother, so as to copy it. When we finally caught sight of the house we were soaked, dirty and weary.

My mother was in the clearing holding something in her hands, not taking her eyes off it. She came cautiously towards us, as if she had sensed our presence. At a distance I thought she had a bowl of fresh cow's milk full to the brim and did not want to spill a single drop, at that time fresh milk was a luxury for our family. David hid behind me and I told him it was my *maman*. We walked on like this and my mother, still staring at her hands, was saying, look, Raj, come and see! I tiptoed up to her, trying to think of some explanation for David's presence, while knowing I could not tell her about the prison. I had never lied to my mother but I could hardly tell her David was one of the prisoners from the Beau-Bassin gaol. Because, when it came down to it, as far as the others were concerned, my father, the policemen, the governor, the very few inhabitants of Beau-Bassin who were in the picture, he was a common prisoner, kept inside high walls round the clock. A bAd mAn, a rUnaway, a rObber.

I was two steps away from my mother. I had certainly not found anything intelligent to say. David sidestepped a little to the right, straightened his back and said: *"Bonjour Madame.* My name is David and I come from Prague."

My mother frowned, looked at me, as if to sound me out and uncover the truth, half opening her mouth, and then an incredible thing occurred, like something out of a fairy story. My mother was holding a red parakeet in her hands. In those days this was a rare bird. While my mother had the power to kill rats, snakes and scorpions with concoctions whose secret she held, she also had the kindness of heart to gather up birds, warm them in her hands and give them a drink in the cup of her palm, patient and gentle, indifferent to the pecking of their beaks. She had rescued this parakeet and I think she had been feeding it on those magic seeds she could produce out of nowhere.

Surprised by David's presence and his words, my mother moved her hand a little and the parakeet took to the air. All we could hear was the beating of its wings and we were dazzled by its vivid red plumage outlined against the blue sky. Like a child's when it is learning to walk, the parakeet's energy flagged a little, it flew lower, circled round and landed on David's head. Just picture it, this majestic bird with its soft, vivid red plumage topped by a bristling crest, with restless black eyes and a tail made up of two or three long feathers like a queen's train, alighting upon David's golden curls, as if, out of our three heads, it had chosen the most inviting.

David froze, his eyes grew round and all he managed to say was: oh oh oh oh and my mother went into peals of laughter. I could not remember when she had last laughed like that, it was certainly when my brothers were still there. My heart rose in my throat and I laughed and wept at the same time, to see the red bird on David's blond head and his terrified expression, to hear my mother's laughter and to realize that, when they died, my brothers had very nearly carried my mother's laughter away with them.

Then the parakeet flew off, making a red trail in the air, to trace the circle we formed, my mother, David and me. It was magnificent and unreal to see it turning and turning like that, as if setting a seal on us, as if blessing us, as if drawing nourishment from us before disappearing, just as if it were a shared dream we were all three of us having at the same time. We did not move, none of us daring to break the imaginary circle, following it with our gaze until it was swallowed up by the blue sky and the green forest.

My mother heaved a sigh, as if to catch her breath and asked me: "Is he your friend?"

Without waiting for my reply she looked at David with great benevolence, as if he had passed through a rite successfully or something of the kind. My mother was one of those women who believe in signs. A red parakeet after a cyclone, a storm-tossed bird regaining its strength and alighting quite naturally on a boy's head before describing circles above three people's heads, this was something my mother could not ignore and I am sure she took it to be a prophecy, a divine promise, a signal from heaven. No questions, no trace of suspicion in her eyes, she welcomed a dirty and tired little boy into her house. I was relieved at the time by her kindly reaction, like a child escaping punishment, but I am well aware of how improbable the situation was. We did not mix with the white people of our country, we hardly ever saw them and I had no friends at school. One must believe that my mother had something else in her heart at that moment.

However, as soon as we entered the house, which was still damp and foul-smelling, I began to feel afraid. The afternoon was declining, the pink tinge to the sky heralded a clear, starry night, but also the arrival of my father. We ate fricasséed rice, sitting on the Mapou stools – that was what we used to call them now we were here at Beau-Bassin. My parents had got them from an old carpenter in the village next to the camp who did woodwork in exchange for the tasks Anil undertook for him, carrying water and wood, and in those days, while the other camp dwellers went on eating their meals seated cross-legged on the ground, we considered ourselves to be blessed and fortunate to be placing our behinds on these coarsely fashioned stools, which sometimes left splinters in our thighs. I believe my mother was feeling the same anxiety as I was, for although she could not know, or did not want to, where David had come from, on the other hand she did know that my father would not like a stranger in our home. Yet every time I caught her eye she smiled at me and her face was serene.

I have said that there was no comparison between our house at Beau-Bassin and our ramshackle hut at Mapou and yet it was wretched too. We had a kitchen and one other room, that was all. My mother and I slept on our mats in this room, myself next to the wall and she, beside me, facing the kitchen. In this room there was a wooden wardrobe where we kept our clothes, our spare sandals, the bedding, and at the back, one of those nooks found only in badly made furniture, where every evening, before my father came home and tried to destroy them, I used to hide my slate, my coloured chalks (white, pink and blue), my sponge, the exercise book with ruled lines between which I could fit my writing and my sums, the pencil, the rubber and my aluminium beaker. The exercise book and the rubber had been given to me by Mademoiselle Elsa at the end of lessons in the previous year to congratulate me on my progress at school.

When I am dead and my son comes to empty my house, he will find a small suitcase on top of my wardrobe crammed with the rubbers which I have amassed throughout my life. On every trip I have made, whether on the island or abroad, I have never been able to restrain myself, I have always bought rubbers of different colours and sizes. My son will be baffled, he will perceive it as an old man's whim. Perhaps I should explain to him that it has been my particular way of frustrating time's attrition, postponing death and sustaining the illusion that one can always erase everything and make a fresh start.

In the kitchen there were nails on the wall for hanging up the copper saucepans, my school bag, and my father's bag. Other utensils were piled on a low wooden table and beneath the only window in the room was the hearth on which my mother cooked.

The house had two doors, one facing north, towards the prison, which we used as the front door and the other opening on to our little makeshift courtyard, which the cyclone had just destroyed. A vegetable bed, a washing-place, a corrugated-iron shed for the wood and tools, washing-lines stretched between the house and the shed, the well just beside it. Beyond that, forest and still more forest. My father used to sleep in the kitchen and that day, when David spent the night at our house, my childhood receded a little further still. My mother took her mat into the kitchen, laid it down beside my father's and when she put us to bed, David and me, she lowered the curtain that separated the two rooms. Ever since our arrival there my mother had always slept beside me and this curtain used to separate us from my father.

I do not need to say much more about that night. I heard my father asking my mother in a loud voice if I was already in bed and then came whispering and a silence which frightened me even more than the cyclone. Clearly I was too young to understand these things and yet, in some part of me, I knew. David was sleeping, exhausted, and I promised myself I would keep my eyes open until the morning, so as to guard against any eventuality, but the child that I was fell into a deep sleep.

The next day was one of those easy and delicious days which life offers unbidden, and I am sure if David were still alive he would have the same blissful memory of that day as me. My mother had cooked rice with milk, sugar and cardamom and, to thicken this breakfast, for there was really very little milk, she had mixed in a spoonful of flour. We ate this happily, David asked for more, my mother scraped the bottom of the pan and David thanked my mother by kissing her on the cheek. I jumped up to do the same and my mother laughed as she had done the day before. After breakfast we set to work to restore the vegetable bed. We dug new furrows, planted cuttings and seeds that my mother had kept, we played games with next to nothing, water, earth, sticks, we ran around the house until we were out of breath, with my mother saying watch out, watch out, and we played at aeroplanes. We went back to our games from the prison, as if we had parted only the day before. No warders or policemen to watch us, we could yell to our hearts' content.

I showed my treasures to David and was very grateful for the way that my new friend respected them so much. After asking my permission, he took the exercise book in his hands and leafed delicately through the pages, as if it had been an ancient Egyptian scroll. We made an excursion into the forest and I taught him how to climb trees. David was made for a noble calling, pianist or poet, not to be a wild boy like me. My body moulded itself to nature, embracing the trees, catching hold of them, I could climb up into a tree in a brace of shakes without even thinking about it. With David it was quite different and it was the first time I had met a boy like this. He would study the tree, walk round it, try to note where you needed to put your foot, where to catch hold of it with your hand, he was an intellectual, that boy.

It was on this day, too, that he showed me his medallion and talked to me about the Star of David, while I, poor fool, poor simpleton, poor kid born in the mud, I was hopping mad. A likely story. And I suppose this forest is called the forest of Raj, eh? How could a star have his name? Could he tell me that? Did he take me for an idiot or what?

My friend gripped his star firmly and told me this David was a king. So what? Raj also meant king!

Very soon the day faded. David found some red and yellow wild flowers that had sprung up just after the cyclone. He picked a bunch of them which he gave my mother when we came back. It was the first time I had seen anyone make such a gift and I remember my mother holding this bunch of flowers in her hand, uncertain what to do with them or else not wanting to be parted from them. There was a hint of red in her cheeks and she wore a timid smile. Even at the age of nine, barely educated and not really *au fait* with the ways of the world, I was bowled over by the beauty of this gesture and I have never forgotten it. I gave my wife flowers the first time we went out together and although this may seem ordinary and not very original today, I can tell you it was quite something in those days, and the girl who went on to marry me some months later had a touch of red in her cheeks, too. I had met her at the public library. She was sitting in front of me when I was preparing, as she was, to take the exams for a teaching diploma and I had first noticed the tiny hairs that traced patterns like commas on the back of her slender neck. At that time she used to gather up her long hair into a chignon and occasionally I had an irresistible desire to blow softly on her neck. I had spoken to her for the first time on the day before the exams and invited her to come and drink a glass of ice-cold milk down at the harbour. I had said that without much hope and was already bracing myself for a refusal, but she looked at me very directly and told me that if she passed her exams she would wait for me at the harbour at eleven o'clock the day after the results were published. She was like that, my wife, she did things step by step, seriously, and I think I fell in love with her that day. As I waited for the exam results I had hopes for myself, I had hopes for her and, in a certain way, I had hopes for both of us. Three months later I put together a bouquet with clusters of roses from my mother's garden, and there she was at the harbour waiting for me.

The second evening, after David and I had gone to bed as on the previous night, we heard my father from a long way off. He was cursing the whole world, coming closer and closer. He was calling to my mother, already threatening her and my name kept recurring in his drunken mouth as well. What was the good of Raj meaning king, what was the good of him giving his son a name like this, at such times Raj was no more than a boy, already terrified, who would soon be cringing under blows.

My mother hurtled into our room, looked at each of us as if she were asking herself which one to choose, quickly bundled up David in a sheet and took him in her arms like a baby. She went out through the back door and set him down beside the stone washing-place. Hide, don't move, she had said wordlessly, soundlessly, just in the trembling of her grown-up's body and a finger placed on her lips.

I have forgotten what I did during those few moments before my father came in wielding a branch he had picked up on the way, for his new bamboo cane had vanished in the cyclone. I was probably praying. I do not know what David was doing, huddled up in the darkness with the ravaged forest all around him, with the cold stone of the washing place against his side, while behind him our tormentor unleashed himself.

It may be that my memory is playing tricks on me, but I am pretty sure my father quite rapidly wearied of us and fell into his alcoholic sleep. Certainly I had felt the bite of the wood on my body, certainly there would be dark-blue marks on my skin as the imprint of my father's violence, like brands applied to animals, certainly I cried my heart out wordlessly because it used to annoy him even more if, by misfortune, a cry or a groan escaped from me and, with time, we had learned to keep our lips sealed and let the tears flow. But that evening it seemed to me that I suffered less and was less afraid than on other occasions, that I was thinking as much of David as of my mother, that, unlike on other occasions, I was not running round like a frightened dog before wetting my trousers and that the whole violent pantomime did not last as long as usual.

10

In the night my mother went out to fetch David and we all three of us slept in the room next to the kitchen. David was shivering and I did not know whether it was from fear or from cold. She put him next to the wall, with me in the middle and herself on the outside. We were silent, fearful and weary. She made both of us drink a hot infusion which tasted of lemongrass and David said thank you to her several times, in a shaky voice, as if he were not just thanking her for the drink but for something else. I have the impression that I went to sleep the second my head touched the mat and I have no need to look far to perceive that my mother was giving us draughts which specifically induced sleep and forgetfulness.

When I opened my eyes my father was already gone, the sun was making a pool of gold in the room and I heard David talking to my mother. I went out and saw them squatting there, arranging some roots, leaves and twigs that my mother had gathered at dawn into a particular order. My mother was slowly reciting the names of the plants and David was repeating them while pretending not to notice my mother's swollen and closed eye. When he saw me he threw himself into my arms and his affection was a marvellous gift that morning. My body was full of aches and pains and my mother prepared a bath of saffron for me with leaves of lilac and some roots. As I remember it, that bath was like a balm anointing the whole of my body. We had decided to go and pick green mangoes for breakfast when suddenly we heard my father's voice at the edge of the forest. My mother rushed over to David and pushed him into the shed we had tidied up the day before. She made a crude bundle of the plants she had just collected and thrust them at David's stomach so that he had no choice but to hold them in his arms, as if he had just caught a football thrown at full speed. I had not known that my mother was so quick-witted. In her place I think I should have run around in circles like a mad dog, incapable of any decision, so much did the sound of my father's voice at that moment affect me like a hammer blow to my head. My mother dragged me out to the vegetable plot and made me crouch down. She took one tail of her sari, lifted it against her face to cover half of it, and gripped the fabric in her teeth. She set to work furiously and I tried to do the same. My father called her. She motioned for me to stay there and went back into the house. I glanced at the shed, at the corrugated iron door simply propped up against it and told myself it must take a superhuman effort for David to remain squeezed in there while the slightest little movement threatened to dislodge the collection of tools, wood and useless objects found here and there, which poor people like us could never resist picking up.

I heard my mother say "out the back" and I pretended to be digging in the earth and then a voice called out: "Is that you, Raj?"

It was one of the policemen from the prison. He was dressed in blue, he had kept his cap on and, seen at such close range in our vegetable garden, he looked like a giant. His truncheon was gleaming and thick. He stared insistently at me and I nodded my head.

"Come here."

Galloping fear gnawed at my stomach, clearly he was there for David, they had found my hiding-place beside the barbed wire, they knew everything and just as I was about to collapse, he pointed his thick finger at my lip.

"What have you got there?"

My top lip was split open and my mother had applied a yellow paste to it. It was my father who replied.

"He had a fall, boss."

His voice was the one I had heard at the prison, hesitant, a womanish voice, as thin as a thread. The policeman turned to my father abruptly and barked: "A fall? Like last time? What do you take me for, warder?"

My father lowered his eyes, laid both hands against his stomach and trembled. It is certainly not pleasant to be reprimanded in front of one's family, but for my father it was a disaster! At that moment I thought he would make us pay for it very dearly. The giant squatted down and, even in this position, he was still taller than me, awesomely impressive. Did he have a wife and son whom he terrorized at night with his hands as big as plates and his arms thicker than my thighs?

"Now then, little one. You were in the hospital a month ago, do you remember?"

"Yes, sir."

"You made a friend, didn't you? David, little David?"

"Yes, sir."

"Good, good. You're a good little boy. Warder! You've got a very good little boy here. Do you know that?"

"Yes, boss."

"Hm. Now tell me, Raj. David hasn't come to see you in the last few days, has he?"

"No, sir."

"Are you sure? You didn't go for a walk near the prison a couple of days ago?"

"No, sir."

The giant stood up, took a few steps around the vegetable plot.

"What a storm eh? I can see you've been working hard. What are you planting there? Eh, young man? Do you know?"

"Yes, sir. There's two rows of tomatoes. Yesterday we planted potatoes and onions. After that you need to ask my mother."

"And you, *madame*. You haven't seen anything?"

"There are some beans as well, and beetroot. But only a few."

"I was asking you whether you haven't seen a little boy here in the last few days?"

"No, sir. What with the cyclone we've been doing nothing but cleaning up and replanting."

I can picture my mother now, a fold of her sari

covering her swollen eye, and I can hear her firm voice. This woman, who was always timid and fearful, lied that day with an aplomb I did not suspect in her. My father, who terrorized his family every day of his life, who lashed out with his feet and hands at us and blew our bodies sideways with his powerful tormentor's voice, this father now stood beside her, shrunk into himself, his eyes on his sandals. How did my mother find such strength?

The policeman glanced at the shed and I prayed that David would make no sound. I looked at my mother and at that moment she turned her head towards me and my father spotted us. His face froze, slowly he turned his gaze towards the shed and I was convinced that he could see right through the sheets of corrugated iron for his eyes grew wider and wider until it seemed to me that they would leap out of their sockets. He was breathing more and more heavily, his shirt rose and fell rapidly, beads of sweat appeared on his face and his fists were clenched.

He knew. He would make us pay very dearly.

The policeman observed the forest and then turned to me: "You're not afraid here, Raj?"

"No, sir."

"Good, good. You could be a policeman one day if you're not afraid. Policemen are never afraid. Isn't that so, warder?"

My father agreed, with a shrill burst of laughter, which the policeman cut off in a flash. This scene has often come back to me at times in my life when I have seen my father drunk and violent. How I have longed to be able to do that, to cut short my father's gestures with a look and, through my presence alone, reduce him to a poltroon who laughed like a woman.

The policeman saluted my mother, touching his cap and then, just like that, without addressing any one of us in particular, he said, in a strong, clear voice: "That little boy is sick. He needs to come back to be looked after."

We waited for a long while after their departure to let David out. He still had the plants in his arms and he was ashen. My mother lifted him up and he remained upright, his body petrified like a tree-trunk. I thought she was going to question me, scold me, but no, she knelt in front of David and asked him: "Where are you sick?"

My mother laid her hands on different parts of his body, the base of his neck, the hollow of his ribs, his heart, his groin, his wrist, the top of his head, and she must have gone into the kitchen to make a mixture of who knows what leaves and roots, ground up together, which she then steeped in water. David swallowed this thick concoction with a grimace. I could not stop thinking about my father's face and it was then, at that precise moment, with David sitting there in a daze, his arms and legs numb, and my mother sitting on the ground too, the bowl empty and marked by a green streak round the rim, left by the mixture, it was at that moment that I decided to run away with David. My mother said nothing. She knew both everything and nothing. We were to some extent caught in a trap and it was my fault. My father would come home that evening, he would search the house and the shed, he would find David, he would take him back, I should be on my own once more, he would beat me until I begged for forgiveness, he would make me pay for everything, the death of my brothers, the shame of being called "warder" in front of us, the humiliation of having revealed to us the face of the affable, obsequious, unimportant employee he was at the prison, he would make me pay for his life of poverty.

It was David who spoke and aroused me from the dazed state I was in. Softly and calmly, he said he would return now, for back there at the prison they were waiting to go to Eretz. Eretz? My mother repeated, with a frown. Then David made a very curious gesture. He plunged two fingers into the earth, then laid them, all covered in soil, against his breast and, his hand upon his beating heart, said Eretz. My mother began weeping softly, because she herself had probably understood that he was speaking of the promised land. I wonder if it was a gesture the Jews at Beau-Bassin regularly made when their hopes faltered as they waited for Eretz.

If my mother had known exactly what it was all about, I mean the war, the extermination of the Jews, the pogroms, if she had known all that, if she had been an educated person, a woman of the world who read newspapers and listened to the radio, if she had been that kind of woman would she have let David go back? And if I, for my part, had known what David had endured for four years, what would I have done? My mother and I did not live in Europe, I know, we had no idea of what was going on, but then that was what a lot of people said: I had no idea of what was going on. Should my mother have asked herself questions? And what of my father in all this? He was a mere prison warder, but he was the first one to rush over to the gate when the bell rang, he was the one who displayed the most zeal when the prisoners had to be hustled back into their quarters . . .These questions haunt me to a degree which numbs me and I know I shall never find any answers.

My mother packed a bag with rice, green fruits to be left to ripen, water, a bottle filled with a green mixture which she made David promise to drink up in less than three days, telling him it was good for malaria. How had she known? Just by laying her hands on him, watching him eat?

I made my own preparations in secret. I took my canvas school bag, slipped three pairs of shorts into it, three shirts, an old sheet, my exercise book, my rubber, my pencil, a kitchen knife, a piece of my father's soap. While my mother was giving her instructions, making copious gestures, and David was listening with the attentiveness of an angel, I went out and left my bag under a tree at the edge of the forest.

I went and sat down beside the vegetable plot and breathed the forest in with all my lungs, the green, ravaged scent of it, its strength as yet hardly resurgent following the cyclone, throwing my head back to open up my chest and it seemed to me that I was inhaling the sky as well, the cloudless blue extent of it. I straightened up my back and let my eyes dwell on the forest's hazy heat, I remember this moment as one of intense concentration, such as I had never known, a recentering of my mind around a single axis: flight. Perhaps, as I have later read in a book, I was determining the course of my fate for the first time.

When my mother and David emerged from the house I felt ready, ready not to cry in front of my mother, whom I was leaving for the first time, and whom I would come back to fetch. I was certain of this, as if it were as easy as fitting your handwriting into an exercise book with ruled lines – I was ready to set off with David towards what I knew best, what was most familiar to me at the age of nine, even though it had taken everything from me: the camp at Mapou.

II

I AM RUNNING WITH GREAT DIF.CULTY. I AM IN a wood and it is as dark as in a closed room, a blockhouse without light, a tomb, perhaps. But I am running, moving forwards and I know I am in a forest, I can smell the scent of the earth, the tart odour of rotting leaves in the darkness, the sugary perfume of the sap infusing the bitterness of the bark. My feet tread on nothing, all I am is a nose, an enormous nose, inhaling all the fragrance of the forest and this is what guides me and I avoid colliding with trees and the wood is immense, I am running, running, running. I am being chased, I know, but I do not know who is chasing me, I just know, without looking behind me, then suddenly I am hiding in a tree, who knows how I climbed up into it so quickly, but there I am and it is such a tall tree, so vast that I have to lean over to see the ground and at length I see them running by, dozens, hundreds, thousands, of policemen, they pass beneath me in a rapid stream, they are absolutely tiny, seen from so high above, but, all the same, I freeze, I do not want them to see me, to smell me, to hear me. They pass at full speed and, despite their uniforms, their caps, their truncheons, they look like ants. I do not stir, I am patient, I am safe.

This is a dream I have often had and when I woke up the feeling of triumph would stay with me for a time, the smells of the forest would persist, yet then, like a bad taste lingering in one's mouth, the bitter realization that it was all illusion would return.

I cannot recall having told David about my plan when we plunged into the forest but it seems to me that he came with me without my having to explain anything at all to him – a naïve notion, I know. It surely cannot be the truth yet it is what my memory tells me, it is what remains sixty years later, perhaps so as to convince myself that I did not force him to follow me. Perhaps it is my only excuse.

I was full of hope, I wanted a brother, two brothers, a family as before, games as before, I wanted to be protected as before, I wanted to catch sight of those shadows out of the corner of my eye that let you know you are not alone. I was struggling desperately to resist everything that took me further away from childhood, I rejected death, rejected grief, rejected separation, and David was the answer to everything.

My idea was to go first to the school and retrieve the map of our country, the one where Mademoiselle Elsa had shown me Mapou with a twirl of her fingers. Lessons had still not started again since the cyclone. When we reached the yard I thought I had taken the wrong path. The two buildings of wood and corrugated iron were spread out there in a dark jumble, like a collapsed house of cards. Chairs and desks smashed to pieces, the grass where the children played had become a dirty brown carpet, in one corner of the yard a kind of pond had formed, studded with mosquitoes, the surface repeatedly rippling with rings. The metal flagstaff was still upright and flying the tattered British flag, in front of which we used to sing "God Save the King" each morning and sometimes, too, on special occasions, we would belt out "Rule Britannia", without understanding a single word of it.

It is a curious thing, memory, as soon as I see a British flag flying, even on TV, the anthem starts up in my head and I cannot help myself. My mind churns out the words, I find it mildly irritating, I want to switch the tape off up there in my old head, but that is how it is, sixty years on, an independent country, a new flag, a new anthem, but when it comes down to it I am one of Pavlov's dogs.

I remember us watching the coloured strips of cloth flapping noisily against the metal, while all around us there was the awesome silence of my school in ruins. Suddenly we heard voices and I cannot say why we bolted, thieves caught in the act would have done no better. David was ahead of me, his feet thumping on the ground, and I followed his fluttering blond hair. I was amazed at his energy, he ran flat out, his body lopsided, his arms flailing the air, as if he were swimming, and me, behind him, with my agile monkey's legs, I was trying vainly to catch up with him and quite soon I, too, was cleaving the air with my arms, I, too, was flinging out my legs in all directions, from a distance we must have looked like two clowns chasing one another. When he turned back, while still continuing his mad run, and observed me, gesticulating like him, we both succumbed to helpless laughter. We dived into the forest, heading towards the village, and there we let our laughter explode in the stifling heat among the trees, until our sides ached. Nothing about this situation was funny, absolutely nothing. We were two completely reckless runaways on an island ravaged by the cyclone, we were two children of misfortune thrown together by a miracle, by accident, what do I know? I believed I was capable of saving him from prison, of keeping him with me, as one keeps a beloved brother, I thought I could banish a little of my mother's grief by bringing her another son, I believed this kind of thing was possible if one truly loved, I was foolish enough to believe that if for no good reason God took away those whom one loves, He would offer something else in compensation. And this something else, evidently, was David. Despite all we had lived through we were still innocent and naïve enough – is that not the magic and drama of childhood? – to laugh at nothing at all.

There was a moment in my life when I discovered the name of the cyclone, but I can no longer recall it today, something like Cindy or Celia, a female name, at all events. I came upon it by chance in a newspaper from 1945 at the archive I like to visit regularly. That is another of my obsessions, delving into old papers. When I went to Europe with my son on one of his business trips I made a round of the archives instead of touring the cities. I was in a cold sweat of excitement in advance, but the naval archives in Vincennes, the ones at the Foreign Office in London and those in Amsterdam disappointed me. It is because I am an old fool accustomed to the disorder, jumble and muddle there is here at home in my own country's archives. Here nothing is protected, they ask you for certain information the first time they see you, but after that they leave you alone, they take no more notice of you, you wander along corridors smelling of old paper, ink and rust, you climb where you can and extract the file that interests you from a stack of them. You can even get locked in there if you are not careful. I once saw a whole family of mice in one corner, I hastened to inform the official who was sitting at the entrance and, without lifting his eyes from his newspaper, he replied in an amused drawl: mice, sir? Is that so? Where was that, then?

It is true, and I agree with all those people who, for years now, have been protesting at the scandal of it, that our country's memory is being lost, as they say, with such incompetents at the archives, and yet when I walked into those white, cream and beige offices and was obliged to fill in a form to state precisely what I was looking for – which I never know in advance, I like delving, discovering, exploring – why I was looking for just this – the question paralysed me – and when I had finally managed to answer all their questions a machine with an automatic arm transferred my document heaven knows where, to a place where there are no families of mice, that is for sure, well, at that moment I felt a pang of nostalgia for my own country's archives. Watching this giant arm through a plate-glass window I felt as if I were in a zoo watching an animal dangerous to man. And then when I sat down with that cardboard box and those beautifully photocopied, carefully protected sheets of paper, with no smell, with nothing, I lost the impulse. I am an old fool, I know, but perhaps my country's thoroughly decrepit archives reassure me, and the older I get the more I like visiting them! That is where I once read the account of that cyclone, described in the newspaper as "devastating", and from it I deduced the date of our escapade: 5 February, 1945.

As we had no choice but to continue without a map, I decided to make for the village and head north from there. I had a vague picture of that map in my head, the red dots scattered here and there, some of them linked by roads (in brown). All around them, mountains (in black), rivers (in white), rectangles of forest or sugar-cane plantations (in green), lakes (in pale blue). Tapping on the map with her bamboo ruler, Mademoiselle Elsa would say: and this is our country. And I believed her. Beau-Bassin was to the south of Mapou, or more or less, so we must go north. The vertiginous height of the mountains, the seething cruelty of the rivers, the ensnaring density of the forests, and the labyrinthine nature of the cane fields, the depth of the lakes and the twists and turns of the roads, none of this was shown on that map. My country was a smooth plain, accessible and coloured to appeal to children. David and I would simply have to follow one of the brown roads, and, with luck, we might be able to ride on a train or the back of a cart. And at Mapou I would not be afraid and, if sadness overcame me at the sight of our camp, the little wood and our rippling stream with its faintly sugary taste, I should have David at my side and soon, my mother. When I think about the hopes I had, I'm bound to wonder whether I was not simply a stupid child. I advanced confidently, stepping over things, skipping along, swinging from branches and leaping energetically, encouraging David who had a method of jumping all his own, as if he were a born long-jump champion. At first he would laugh, which made me laugh too, then he began to run, awkwardly, of course, and then, when there was every indication that he was going to collapse pathetically, with a firm thrust of his left foot against the ground he was up and away, his legs flailing the air, his arms above his head, happy, so happy, almost flying, to come to earth several yards further on where, in advance, I had checked that there was only welcoming moss and earth. At every clearing we crossed he did his big number for me and each time he was in the air his face was turned towards me and this reminded me of my big brother Anil, turning back towards Vinod and myself in the little wood at Mapou when we heard the stream, and it was the same affection that I read in his features, the same way of asking are you happy? Does this give you pleasure?

In the forest did I forget why we were there, David and I? Did I forget the policeman, his gleaming truncheon, his voice when he came looking for David? Did I forget my father's sweating face, his eyes infused with rage when he looked at us, my mother and me? So is that all it took, a few games, this illusory freedom for us boys – shouting and laughing uproariously, leaping and scrambling everywhere – is that all it took for me to forget what I had promised him, for me to lose my way? For suddenly the forest stopped, its dense green protection came to an end and we found ourselves on the verge of a neat, smoothly packed earth road, incongruous after that cyclone. I remember clearly that the road was down below us and, in continuation of our wild flight, we jumped down from the embankment, feet first, happy, proud and strong, and this terrible road was as smooth as one imagines the roads in paradise, but it led straight up to a locked gate with padlocks and chains, surmounted by a sign which, like the road, seemed to have been spared by the storm and bawled out in its bold, clear lettering: *Welcome to the State Prison of Beau-Bassin.*

David emitted a cry – shattered happiness, shattered dream – turned back, hurling himself against the embankment to scale it, grasping at roots and branches and our joy, our energy, our strength and our pride had all suddenly vanished and the earth gave way beneath his feet in great clods.

What happened after that managed to shatter the fragile innocence that had enveloped us since the outset of our flight. I could no longer find my way and it felt to me as if nature, hitherto asleep, benevolent, welcoming, had gone onto the alert, was on the defensive. The trees pressed close together, the earth gave way beneath our feet, uprooted tree-trunks barred our way, we found ourselves in humid, rotting areas, without light, we allowed ourselves to be drawn along false trails and found ourselves in culs-de-sac, menaced by gnarled trees where, amid mingled branches and foliage, we imagined the faces of monsters and devils. With trembling bodies and beating hearts we would stop to listen to sounds we thought we had heard. We slipped, we stumbled, the brambles attacked us, our bags which previously had remained firmly slung across our shoulders and our chests now began to cut into our flesh and became caught on bushes, tugging us abruptly backwards. And three times we were revived by wild hope on discovering a forest edge close by and three times we were slapped in the face by the terrible, smooth, neat road that led to the prison. And three times, the same truth: we were rUnaways and henceforth that was where we belonged.

When we finally found our way, thanks to who knows what miracle, and I saw the great rock painted white which marked the entrance to the village, we were nothing more than two frightened, trembling animals. I realized that we had made no progress, that dusk was at hand and it had taken us a whole afternoon to travel a distance that used to take me half an hour weighed down with a bundle of linen!

For the first time I thought about going back home. What awaited me there seemed to me less fearsome than what I had just lived through and I thought it would be the same at the prison for David. This appalling and shameful notion which came into my head, those few moments when I had the urge to take him back there, all this is what I should be confronted with now, and let there be no doubt about it. I did not want to get David out of the prison because he was unhappy, no, I wanted to get him out because I was unhappy. A few hours in the forest had been enough to reduce my generous impulse to tawdry bravado.

Just beyond the white stone, round the bend in the road, we were about to see Madame Ghislaine's white house with its red dahlias. I put an arm round David's shoulders – there he was, trembling with the shudders of a wounded animal, his bones sticking out, as mine did, how could I have thought for a moment, a single moment, of taking him back? – I was helping him duck down, so as to walk past the dressmaker's bamboo hedge, but there was no house any more, no dahlias, and no bamboos in the place where sometimes in the past this woman, who loved Jesus the son of God above all, had shown me sparrows' nests and their eggs speckled with brown, with all the patience and wonder of someone showing off the handiwork of Jesus, the son of God himself. The hedge had been crushed by a giant foot, what was left of Madame Ghislaine's house was three wooden walls. The roof blown away, the canopy with its friezes and the posts of the verandah, where she sometimes waited for me, all blown away. In the yard an iron bedstead overturned, clothes caught up here and there, one or two saucepans, splintered wood everywhere and as I walked round the shattered house I saw the black sewing machine, smashed and wrecked, on the ground.

The whole village was like this, flattened, and I thought of our tiny house, square and deep in the forest, which, for its part, had survived. The hedges that shielded the villagers' houses from prying eyes, the trees that were sometimes so laden with fruit that they seemed to be leaning extra low, so as to be relieved of their burden, the flowers, the vegetable beds, the shade for resting in, the sunlight for drying the linen, all had vanished. As in the school yard, the devastation was accompanied by a deep and frightening silence. No-one was weeping over their houses, their possessions, there was just the wide-open sky and I thought about what my father had told us when he returned home after those days in the prison, the litany of the names of missing persons on the radio.

We found a corner sheltered from the wind. We shared bread and fruit and David drank his green mixture conscientiously. I thought about my mother and I had to clench my teeth and hug my knees to my chest so as not to go running to her. Darkness enveloped us and I was losing my self-assurance and confidence, the difficulty of the task was only too clear to me. Doubt, fear and the absence of my mother weighed heavily on me, and it was only the promise I had made and David's presence – an indescribable combination of affection, simplicity and duty, yes, somewhere I felt I had a duty to him, had I not brought him home with me and now, here, what would my brothers have said if they had known me to be so cowardly? – that stopped me taking him back.

Why did I talk about Mapou that night? To give

myself fresh confidence, to compensate for the longing to be with my family? To help David forget that terrible time in the forest, to give him a promise of sunlight and blue sky? I filled up that dark night with words, with a story, the only one I really knew, the story of Mapou.

I remember David's legs were covered in scratches on which the blood had dried and he had let them fall, flat on the ground, with not even the strength to bring them up to his chest. Painfully, we carried the remains of the metal bed over to our corner for protection. I remember the sewing machine, the way it was twisted, smashed, wrecked. I remember that courtyard in the old days, always so well maintained, those vivid dahlias of which all that remained was a heap of mud. And this silence, different from the one that reigned in the forest. In the forest it is an almost animal silence, where nature lies in wait, ready to spring, a dense silence, its surface interrupted by snapping sounds, rustling, presences. Here it was a desolate silence, with only the wind blowing through inanimate things.

To begin with I talked about the good things at Mapou, the sugar canes you could chew and suck at will, the stream, the weddings celebrated after nightfall when everyone lit terracotta lamps, which gave the camp a festive air, games with my brothers –

but very quickly there was this knot being drawn tighter and tighter, rising in my throat and I have no more to tell of things, fine and gay I can only think about the storm, the rain, the thunder and the stream turning into a torrent. Did I tell him about the fear in my belly, my elder brother's white shirt and his voice shouting come on come on come on and that fear exploding when the shirt disappears and the voice falls silent, and the rain redoubles and the thunder keeps rumbling, and did I tell him how my little brother and I yelled his name, our elder brother's name – that perfect brother who loved his stick, one end of which was a U, that brother who played at aeroplanes with me? In our lives we had seen very few aeroplanes flying over our heads and then everyone would come out of their huts and children would jump up and down, shouting AER-O-PLANE, AER-O-PLANE, hoping to reach the flying machine just by jumping like that, that is why we loved playing at aeroplanes so much. And did I tell him how suddenly I had no brothers and there was only me, no more elder brother, no more little brother, no more three of us, in short, no brothers any more, just me, the weakest link, shouting Anil, Vinod, Anil, Vinod, and did I tell him about Vinod's body, about throwing the stick into the water, could I have told him all that, from start to finish, without leaving anything out, without forgetting anything?

And David's eyes wet with tears and his questions, David did not understand, he got everything mixed up, he said only one body, two brothers, why just the stick and not him, not your brother, why didn't they find him, *maybe he's still alive your elder brother*, did he really say that, David, he who had lost everything and who had seen what he had lost had seen the stiff bodies no longer moving he had those pictures in his head he knew what death was he had been rubbing shoulders with it for four years, but my brother my big brother I had only seen his stick but the stick wasn't him was it and what if your brother's still alive did David really say those words what if your brother's still alive words that opened my heart and my head it felt as if the sunlight had just entered in there what if your brother's still alive what if your brother's still alive words that made me leap words that made me cry for I was convinced of it and I had uncovered God's design He whose ways are as my mother had told me relating things which seem unjust or incomprehensible to us but which have a purpose and I had understood this purpose and in my head everything was clear God had put David in my path and the prison and the policeman and the cyclone to oblige me to go back to Mapou for my brother was waiting for me there we had evidently left so quickly how could he have known we were here and all this finally made sense just wait till my mother hears this Anil still alive my elder brother the one who caught my mother's head when she fell and who took a beating instead of me what if your brother's still alive these words made me sad and euphoric at the same time for it does not take much for one to believe that the dead can return you do not have to be a child for this it is enough to be very unhappy and at that moment in that dense dark night amid the ruins of Madame Ghislaine's house with the wind howling and while a moment before I had been afraid of this dead village this ghost village my courage returned and determination pulsed once more in my veins the imminent joy of finding Anil once more whistled in my ears and I hugged David tightly in my arms I jumped I shouted and he did the same David he jumped with his long-jump champion's legs his legs scratched and scarred by the forest and in his language he began singing a song of happiness in which he clapped his hands and I remember I was never in time I was a beat behind and my hands were clapping when he had already finished the refrain but David did not hold it against me he closed his eyes and it seemed as if this song this melody this prayer in that language in which all I could catch was shushing and words ending in *shem* came from far away and when he shut his eyes like this he became someone else a boy come from far away a boy remembering what he has been and while he held both my hands and we danced round in a circle of happiness I wonder if he knew why I was suddenly happy excited impatient energetic how I had swiftly passed from dejection to alertness that evening for if I could have run all the way to Mapou carrying him on my shoulders I should have done it what did David truly think about it I think he was happy to be here, there, now and to give me pleasure, to follow me, to do like me, not to imitate me but to learn from me while God knows I had nothing to give how sad it is at the age of nine to have no gift to offer and there he was watching me with his big eyes turning from green to grey keeping me company in my frail and crazy happiness his eyes which expected so much of me what did I do my God what did I do with that hope what did I do?

12

I WAS EXPECTING THAT, AT MY GREAT AGE, I should take an indulgent view of my life, knowing that regrets serve no purpose, that you need a lot of luck to fulfil your dreams, that the best way to live is to do your utmost at every moment and that so many things happen without us, even though we spend all our time scurrying like madmen, in the belief that we can make some difference. But when I recall those summer days in 1945, when I speak of David, my heart is heavy, my head teems and I am so assailed by regrets that I could weep.

I so wish David could have had the chance to grow up and grow old like me. I should have liked him to tell his story himself in his own words and with the things that he alone could see. He might be saying things like: *On the other side of the barbed wire I saw a dark boy with black hair. He was weeping like me and he had leaves stuck to his face and you could have taken him for an animal. He was half buried in the earth, this boy with a dusky skin. I could only see his head, his eyes as black as billiard balls, and if he'd not been weeping he would have frightened me with his face like a savage's.*

Perhaps he might also say: *Raj taught me how to climb trees, how to run so that my feet don't touch the ground (or hardly), he told me to run for the sake of running, to forget your body and your head and just feel the air against your face, feel the speed you can reach the more you forget your legs and look straight ahead and laugh.*

Did he think I was going to lead him to Eretz? Did he think we were going to a place where we could have been happy or did he – what a terrifying question at my age – make that journey simply for my sake? From his life as a solitary, a deported Jew, an orphan, a prisoner, a child deprived of childhood, a child with too good and close an acquaintance with death, David had, I believe, learned to cease to exist, to forget he had a heart that could do anything other than weep, arms, legs to run with and such a sweet face that one could do nothing but cherish it. He had forgotten all this, forgotten he was made of flesh and blood, forgotten he had the potential to grow up and be a man. But who am I to be telling all this today, to be saying all this, to be talking about him like this, as if I had some kind of right to speak of these appalling things, what do I know of how he might have felt, what do I know of deportation and pogroms, what do I know of prison? I am just a poor old man!

Did I keel over just then? My son is here, helping me to get up, picking up my stick, taking my arm. He talks to me, but I can hardly hear him, I can hardly see him. He leads me to a bench, beneath a tropical almond tree, a few yards away from David. I resist and my son says have a bit of a rest, the sun's very hot, you can go back in a little while. There is such tenderness for me in his voice that I give in. The shade does me good, he hands me a bottle of cold water and sits down beside me. He asks me if I knew personally someone buried here and I nod. I cannot take my eyes off David's grave and perhaps that is why my son respects my silence and says nothing more to me.

It is too late now, sixty years too late, to be realizing here, in front of his grave, that David had forgotten how to be himself, had ceased to be a little boy and that everything he did was for me, so as to live a biy through me, for, having seen himself robbed of his own life, he perforce did not know how to do otherwise. During those few days we spent together did I help him to rediscover himself? No. For the next morning it was all about my story. It was my brother I was setting out to find, this was the priority that counted and no longer the fact that David had escaped from prison, that I had gagged him with my wrist when he tried to help a friend, that I had taken him home, that I had aroused in him hopes for a life of freedom, that I had dreamed up the idea of this flight all on my own and had imposed it on him. It was my own happiness that was at stake. I hope he will pardon me the shamelessness of this.

My memories have been in ferment for a long time and sometimes I have my doubts about them. I have such vivid pictures in my mind that I feel as if I had seen them yesterday morning. I recall our long walk the next day on the earth road that skirted the forest and which we stuck to, so as to postpone going back among the trees, that dirty earth road, the thick mud with a cracked surface which had formed along each side, the branches, the leaves, the dead birds, as if a part of the forest had come here to die, its last gasp henceforth laid out beneath our footsteps, and there we were, like good children, prudently walking on the left, when we could have made this road into our playground, into a world of our own, trampling on it, turning it upside down, but no, we walked along in a straight line, like soldiers. Before and behind us the same landscape stretched away endlessly. A strip of nature devoid of life. Sometimes I thought I saw a fruit that had been spared, I would stoop, pick it up, examine it, but ended by throwing it away, for mangoes, lychees, pawpaws, longans, all these summer fruits had been mown down at the height of their ripeness and were nothing but rotting husks, sticky balls, dripping wet and stinking. I showed David how to test the quality of a fruit, to sniff a mango at its base, roll a lychee in his hand, squeeze a longan between thumb and finger to check the softness of the skin. He listened to me, followed my instructions seriously, then flung out his arm behind him and hurled the fruit even further than me, yet again, perhaps, a way of telling me how much he was with me, how much he agreed.

"Listen."

It was David who murmured this and I stopped, cocked an ear. Further on, a noise. Muffled conversations, directions to work faster, to turn left, turn right, stop. I took David's hand and we went on walking, all our attention now on the noise, and the notion came to me of a town with horse-drawn carriages. But it was a house we came upon, lying across our road. It was white, vast, made of bricks, with all the joints visible. I had never seen anything like it. The houses of the bosses at Mapou were much less grand. I remember I began counting the windows and there was the same number on each façade. The earth road stopped some fifty yards from the house and after that the path was paved with stone. There were two horses dragging tree-trunks, bundles of bamboo, foliage and branches, they moved forward unhurriedly, their heavy hooves clip-clopping, while a very old man, dressed like those at the Mapou camp, a piece of fabric around his loins, was watching to see the load did not fall off. All around the house men were digging ditches to replant tall bamboos. The earth and mud that came out of these ditches was piled up in wicker baskets, and two little boys no taller than ourselves were carrying them over to a cart and the mud trickling through the wickerwork stained their legs. Women emerged regularly from the house and flung buckets of water into the yard, making reddish-brown spray.

I do not know who noticed us first. The men stopped digging, the women set down their buckets, put their hands on their hips, the two boys set down their baskets and the old man stopped keeping watch over the loading. Only one of the horses went on stamping its hooves.

A young man dressed in English style, canvas trousers, shirt, jacket and shoes gleaming with black polish, appeared. He was a mestizo, with blue eyes. But in those days, so far as I knew, there were only whites, blacks and Indians upon the earth. To me this man, with his bronze skin, sky-blue eyes and frizzy golden hair, this walking cocktail, looked like an extraterrestrial. He came up to us and I saw that he held a pair of gloves in his left hand. He looked at us attentively and stifled a guffaw. I have never known why. Was it because we were dressed like diligent scholars, with our blue shorts, our white shirts and our satchels over our shoulders, was it our scratched faces, our savage look, or was it the way we were holding hands, firmly, without trembling?

To my great surprise he offered us work. He addressed David in French, saying that there would be three coins and some food if we would lend a hand, and I was the one who replied. The man was still staring at David, who did not flinch. Never refuse work, our elders say, not ever.

"Yes. We'll work."

We left our bags on a reclining chair under the porch and picked up wicker baskets. The men shovelling mud and earth into the baskets looked at us pityingly. At first they did not fill the baskets to the brim as they did for the other boys, but even so I should never have imagined earth and mud could be so heavy. One of the boys showed us how to wedge the basket on your hip, but this was a weight utterly different from that of a bucket of water or a bundle of clothes. The slime trickled down our legs, twigs worked loose from the plaited wickerwork and stuck into our flesh, the baskets slipped, fell onto our feet, spilling all the mud over us. Then, just like that first time when I caught sight of David through the barbed wire, we exchanged glances and understood one another without uttering a word, we did the work together, each taking one side of the basket, walking sideways like crabs, then swinging the load to give it momentum and hurling the mud onto the cart. Everyone stared at us curiously, as if the idea of getting together and combining forces had never occurred to them.

After a score of basketfuls they gave us lunch. Slices of bread spread with margarine, sardines in oil, bananas and sugared water in real glasses. It was the first time I had experienced anything like that. All the workers, children and adults, were sitting in a corner, some on a rock, some squatting on their heels, some on the pavement itself. We ate in silence, out of total respect for our hunger, our aching muscles and our hard work. Perhaps I had the fleeting impression of being a man, of having worked and earned my meal. I felt stronger, more confident, I thought about saving a piece of bread, but I was too hungry and so was David. When he had finished eating David walked over to the verandah to take his medicine from the bag. I had my back to him, still basking amid this new community, this brotherhood of workers, but I heard him running across the paving stones.

"Raj, Raj, Raj."

I knew that tone of voice of David's. It was the tone he used the day they removed me from the hospital. I stood up abruptly and saw a long, black, gleaming car approaching the house. A man said: "Watch out. It's the boss."

I certainly knew this big car. It was often in the prison compound, it was outside when the Jews were demonstrating, it was the governor's. David was running with our two bags and when he drew level with me I began running too. One of the workers, a faceless, voiceless man, to whom we had not spoken, lunged with both hands and tried to catch David. He could only get a hand to one of the bags, halted David in full flight. I remember David's body jerking backwards, his mouth opening in an O, his eyes popping out. And now I go back, I grasp David by one arm and pull, yelling all the while. Why am I shouting like this? David is being choked by the strap and I am trying to free him. The man continues to hang on to him, he has a grimace on his face which I take to be a smile and this is intolerable to me and

I suddenly become a monster, uttering shameful oaths which I do not even understand, which grate on my tongue and my throat, ones I had heard at the camp, long ago, ones my father utters when he emerges from the forest completely drunk and gets ready to beat his wife and son, I fling these appalling things at this man hanging on to David who opens wide his eyes confronted by my verbal battery, and now at this moment I am no longer a child, here on these muddy paving stones I take my leave of little Raj, the naïve dreamer. It is sad and it is hard to say it, but at this moment I am well and truly my father's son.

The car stops, the door swings open, causing a flash of sunlight across his black skin, the strap of the bag breaks, the bottle containing David's medicine, which my mother had prepared with her magic touch and her miraculous herbs, shatters, vomiting its fragments of glass and its green mixture across the paving stones in the shape of a star, and we run, we run, we run, pursued by the shouts of the mestizo. He yells out our names and this frightens us so much we plunge back into the forest and with a rustle of leaves, its denseness closes behind us.

13

AS WITH ANIMALS, FLIGHT SHARPENED OUR senses. I saw everything, spotting well in advance where to leap, where to duck, anticipating where to swerve to the left, increasing speed at the right moment and, like a sprinter, gaining momentum, lengthening my stride, above all one must keep going, never stop. I could hear David behind me and we were making identical movements which produced identical sounds, right down to the swift, panting of our breath. A branch would crackle as I passed, a handful of seconds later it crackled again as David passed; when we crossed ground covered in moss there was the same muffled sound beneath our sandals. David was my shadow more than ever, the echo of my slightest move, my mirror image, sometimes reassuring, sometimes intolerable, for I could not shirk responsibility for my decisions now, down to the smallest, the tiniest, the most trivial. Every move I made was imprinted twice in my memory. When we heard the muted sound of water we hardly slowed down but simply veered towards it, unquestioningly, thinking of nothing else. We plunged into this dirty, heavy, murky water. It was freighted with everything that had not withstood the cyclone, but we drank greedily, closing our eyes.

I must be forgiven now. All this, and especially what follows, has been with me for so long. It has all been fermenting amid other memories and the time to speak of them is now or never, I cannot shirk it once again. I am frightened, I am seventy and my memory frightens me! What I want is to tell *precisely* what happened, it is the least I can do for David, I want to tell what matters, I want finally to put him at the centre of this story, I want him to be an individual, to have space to speak of his grief, his sorrow, yet David never talked about these things, he had not learned to think about himself, to say, as I could: I miss my brothers, I'm cold in the forest, I'm afraid, I want to go home to my mother.

At the time I did not understand this, he was a wonderful companion for me, I admired his peaceful presence, his unsuspected strength, I told myself that he was braver than me, that he was made of the same stuff as my brothers, his way of doing exactly what I expected of him, his way of sacrificing himself for me, of not disappointing me. Not for an instant did it occur to me that he had quite simply never learned to think about himself and that he had been shaken by so many deaths, by such misfortune that his body, his heart, his head no longer existed. He moved through life as if he knew that what had happened to his family would catch up with him, he sang his songs, learned who knows where, I like to think it was his mother who put those words into his mouth, he sometimes talked very fast and now I understand that he was holding on to Yiddish, his mother tongue, because this was all that was left to him. His language was a kind of music for me and, when night fell in the forest, he sang, as some of them did in the evening at the prison, they sang to set themselves free from the island they detested, this country which for them would always be a prison.

I remember I one day ordered one of those language-learning books, *Pocket Yiddish* it was called. I had seen an order form in a magazine and, without really thinking about it, I had sent off a postal order. I waited for two months and when the parcel finally arrived I put it on the kitchen table without being able to open it, my hands were shaking so much. It felt to me as if this parcel contained a little of David, of my childhood, of those summer days when sometimes, if David was vainly trying to tell me something, he would become irritated and his first language would find its way to his tongue again. My wife opened the parcel for me and put it into my hands. It was a small book and I was disappointed. The parcel had seemed large because it was lined with bubble wrap. I pressed the book to my heart and then had the bright idea of turning to the final pages first, like people who start reading books from the end because they cannot stand the suspense. There was a French-Yiddish vocabulary. I looked up the words for "brother", "hunger" and "mother", and my vision was clouded with tears. I closed the book, never to open it again, for I had been trying to read aloud and the shushing sounds coming from my mouth touched a chord in my memory and I found it unbearably sad.

It seems as if all I can recall of that stream is its turbulent brown colour and, despite this, the incredibly sweet sensation when it poured into us to quench our thirst. We followed its course for a short while and when I was sure that there was nothing but a curtain of silence around us, that we would not be caught by the mestizo we stopped.

It is surprising how the body can suddenly change

into an enemy that has to be subdued, tamed. Had we not been running a moment before, fleeing, in full possession of our faculties, our bodies obeying us like slaves? And now comes this numbness, then shooting pains all along your legs that make you feel as if someone were ripping a vein out, weak, trembling knees that make you fall to the ground, you are gasping for breath, raw, it sticks in your throat, desperately you force your mouth open, your face turned towards the sky, the taste of blood on your tongue, the feeling that your heart has swollen so much it is beating not just in your chest but in your stomach, your back, your shoulders, your head, your ears. A little to the right of us the ground rose and we chose to take a path which wove its way up through the trees rather than go downhill with the river. We found a grassy and leafy spot a few yards further on and from there the purling of the water made a pleasant sound and we collapsed with weariness.

I remember the smell of the earth glutted with too much water from the sky, and that of the leaves rotting and giving off an acid aroma, I remember the opaque blue of the sky seen through the leaves of the trees, I can picture the shadow playing over David as he lay on his back, his mouth open, and if I looked hard at his chest I could see the steady pulse of his heart against his shirt. My body was heavy, weary, and

I felt as if it were sinking into the earth as slowly and surely as into a quicksand.

To tell *precisely*. When I awoke nothing had changed, the blue and green pattern above my head, the stream in the distance, the dampness of the soil, the gentle warmth of a peaceful awakening after a well-earned rest. There was just a slightly sour smell now mingled with that of the saturated earth. Still lying there, I turned my head to the right where David was sleeping. He was no longer there. How to tell *precisely* the shock I had? My heart leaping out of my chest and thumping against my ribs, that is the feeling. The whole of me rearing up, standing upright, yelling David!

Where he had been there was a trail of vomit. *Precisely*, yes? David had brought up onto the leafy ground everything he had gulped down after that work at the governor's, the bread, the banana, the sardines. I could see he had been swallowing it whole, hardly chewing it, and it was quite agonizing to me to think of it, David gulping everything down like a starved child.

I raced down the slope yelling his name and it was as if I were reliving my life over and over again, as if that were my fate, to be left behind while the others vanished, and this made me cry out even more, in terror, in fury. David was lower down, bent over the stream and I fell upon him, kissed him, hugged him tightly and felt his burning skin. He seemed to me to have grown thinner than he had been just now but maybe this was due to his expression. He stared at me as if he were emerging from a dream and wondering who I was. I supported him up to the spot where we had slept and retrieved my bag. There was now a cloud of flies buzzing around the little mound of vomit and David turned his head away. I still had a thumping heart, but I was no longer frightened. I had found David again.

We walked until we came to a low wall built of stones so white it was as if they were made of sand. We turned to the left, for in the other direction the forest was growing more dense. The ground was becoming stony and I could feel the sharpness of the pebbles beneath my sandals. David was behind me, with one hand on the wall, the other on the small of his back, but he was not complaining. When the forest opened out and the wall stopped, a broad plain unfolded before us. It was green, dense and, as dusk fell, it seemed to grow even darker. A little over to the right there was a town, and I looked at David as I pointed it out to him. I did not know where we were, we had run so much in all directions, but the sight of this town, these houses and a road cutting the plain in two, reassured me. Tomorrow we would go down there, tomorrow we would manage better. Tomorrow we would find the road to Mapou. The sky had turned pink as the light faded. The plain did not seem to bear any scars from the cyclone. It was calm, like a great animal lurking in silence and we paused in silence for a moment on the brink of this steep hill.

Then we stepped over the little wall and, to our great surprise, found ourselves in a kind of orchard. I cleaned the ground beneath a camphor tree as best I could and settled David there. He leaned against the trunk and closed his eyes. I took a clean shirt and pair of shorts out of the bag and put them down beside him before going off to look for food. It was quite a fine orchard, further on there were little ravenales, scarcely taller than I was, planted in a straight line, pineapples here and there, a few Chinese guava trees, breadfruit trees, and giant cactuses at the foot of which red flowers were rotting. I picked two pineapples and some green guavas, I filled my bottle by collecting the water that had gathered among the ravenale leaves. On my return David had changed and he had tried to bury his soiled clothes beside him. I pretended not to have noticed.

David had not said a word since the stream, his eyes had a grey, glazed look and he was shaking with fever. When he tried to get up the pain made him grimace. I massaged his legs, copying my mother's actions, and his skin beneath my hands was flaccid and trembling. It was nothing, just a fever, how many times had I lain, trembling, on a bed of fever, and yet there I was, no? I said this to David as I massaged his legs and the soles of his feet. That night David drank some water, but he ate nothing. When it was completely dark we covered ourselves with the sheet I had brought. We sat with our knees against our chests, with our backs against the camphor tree which, now that the sun had gone, was exuding all its sugary fragrance, and the fine coverlet was drawn up round our shoulders. The sky was a carpet of stars and I felt safe here. This was the night when David sang and now I am in the winter of my life, and can in all honesty confront what I did, what happened to me, what I deserved or otherwise, I can say that for me his singing was one of the most magnificent things I have ever heard.

At the prison hospital I used to hear these same laments in Yiddish and it seemed to me that they came from people's hearts at that same time of day, when all is dark and the stars are out, when the Jews were alone and could do no other than confront their own lives and hold fast to what they had been in the past. Someone would begin the singing and others would join in, never very loud, never at the tops of their voices, never in protest, just a murmuring through the lips, a caress on the tongue, a bare melody, softly brushing the vocal cords, and apart from this, apart from this music that hovered over that prison with its dirty, ignoble walls, nothing stirred, and it was like a secret they were sharing which linked them from note to note, from refrain to refrain. I was amazed that even the weakest of the weak sang, from the depths of their beds, but, after all, perhaps they, the ones who were most sick, were the ones who needed it most.

David's little voice arose beside the camphor tree, his Yiddish words filled that tropical night, his Jewish song enfolded the forest and enfolded me, little Raj. His voice was so serene, the words flowed naturally and this rosary entered into me and reached my heart, making me at one with the world around me, as if, until then, I had been a stranger to it. This lament seemed to enhance the beauty of the natural world and, if I may dare say it, amid these recollections, amid these terrible and barbaric events, I felt as if this lament spoke of the beauty of life itself. Even though I did not understand a single word of it, the tears rose to my eyes and, more than everything, more than those days spent together, more than our escapade itself, it was this moment that tied for ever the knot which bound us together.

14

WE SPEND OUR DAYS TRYING TO READ THE lines of nature. I believe men have been like this from time immemorial, on the look-out for answers, signs, warnings, punishments and rewards which come from the beyond. When I awoke next morning a pale and almost milky-blue sky lay open above us, dew glistened on the branches, the birds had returned and were chattering in the orchard, a golden light like a halo surrounded us with gentle warmth and I felt as if David's singing had kept me company in my dreams and he had created this marvellous morning. David was on my right and his silence conveyed that he was in contemplation like me, drinking in the freshness of this new dawn and all it promised. I remembered the valley and the town lower down and I felt ready for that day of walking, was not this marvellous morning a sign of renewal for us? If I had had but the least foreknowledge of the terrible day we were to live through, if I had had but the slightest warning – a crow perched above us, a black cloud scarring the sky, a wild boar grunting among the trees, a bitter wind blasting away all those shining stars of the dew – I should have found a hiding-place, dug a ditch with my bare hands and, with David beside me, I should have curled up, rolled into a ball and hidden in silence, as I used to, hoping and praying that ill luck would pass us by and not notice us. But nothing of the kind occurred. The sky remained untarnished, the birds flitted about in the trees, the leaves rustled in the gentle breeze and caused the light to tremble. I suddenly thought about my mother and my heart closed up with grief like the leaf of a sensitive plant when touched. During those days I forced myself to subdue thoughts that came too close to my mother. I knew that thinking about her would mean thinking about my father and what he was capable of and what had been happening in our house deep in the woods since I had run away and taken David with me. It was David or my mother. David or going home.

I convinced myself and throughout the day repeated

to myself that I was going to get to Mapou, that Anil would be there and my mother would join us, that David would be a brother for us, a son for my mother, and that we should be three brothers once more, that things would go better. I know now that this scenario was ridiculous, that it derived from a few words of David's I believed I had heard, because the heart longs for miracles, and yet during those hours of flight, nothing was more real or tangible to me.

To rid myself of thoughts of my mother and the feeling of missing her, I stood up abruptly and a terrible stiffness spread along my spine and into my neck. It was not really a pain, it felt as if a tree-trunk had been attached to my back and I had got up bearing the weight of it. This took my breath away and I fell back onto my knees. David had stood up as well but he stayed with his back leaning against the tree, his lips pale and drained of blood, with shining eyes he looked at me on the ground and held out his arm to me. I do not know if this was a cry for help or if he wanted to hold me back. I paused quite a while before standing up again and took a few steps to try to unloose the stiffness in my body. I drew great breaths, made movements with my arms and after a moment the weight was eased without really disappearing. We ate some slices of pineapple and drank water. Once my bag was restocked with a bottle of water and some fruit we began our descent into the valley.

Walking was painful for David, but he was moving forward. I found a stick not far from the orchard and David used it as a walking-stick. I told myself it might be the branch of a camphor tree, like Anil's, and this pleased me, it was encouraging, like another sign that my brother was waiting for us, that the day would go well. The way down to the valley was endless. Yet the direction was clear, we could not go wrong. We slithered on loose stones, sharper than the day before, and more numerous, could that be possible? It seems to me that we walked for an hour before the valley came into view and I now had to struggle against a longing to stretch out full length, to unburden myself for a while of this anvil that lay across my spine, crushing the back of my neck and squeezing my head in a vice.

The town looked to me quite close and, without stopping, we took the footpath that wound down into the valley towards the right. David was breathing with difficulty, he was burning hot and sweating and his hair, plastered across his brow and the top of his head, looked less blond. Ever since the previous evening I had been asking him the same question. Are you alright? Are you alright? Are you alright? Sometimes he said yes, sometimes he nodded, sometimes he contented himself with smiling, but now, just before the descent into the town, he shook his head, slowly from left to right, from right to left.

"No."

He found it hard to keep his eyes open, as if the daylight troubled him. It was at this moment that I began to feel afraid. I did not say any more, we walked arm in arm until the track became flat and less stony. It was slightly sloping and my leaden body belied my memories: no, I could never have been that swift and supple lad whose favourite sport was running downhill, for if you accelerate in the right way and keep looking in front of you to spot obstacles, it feels as if you are growing wings. I had entwined my arm around David's. I could feel regular shivers beneath his skin and this made a greater impression on me than outright shaking. It seemed to me a far cry from the time when David used to do his run-up and take to the air, his legs flailing like a champion's. I pictured again his face in mid jump. That face fixed only on me and I understood then, deep inside me, that for us this kind of simple, uncomplicated joy was at an end.

I shall try to describe precisely the place where we stopped. This is important because it is the place where David closed his eyes. I do not know if he died there or later, on my back. I do not know and, to tell the truth, I have no desire to know, for some things are so painful that they are best left in peace. And even when you are old, like me, and you know the sum total of grief a whole lifetime unloads upon you, when you have enough wrinkles and blurred memories to believe that henceforth everything will be clear, yes, even now, I have no desire to know.

We had not made much headway, that is certain, but it was like entering a parallel world, so different was it from the one we had been in before. There were tall trees with immense trunks and roots that emerged from the ground to form mounds covered in moss. On some of these trunks grew long, supple ferns. Shafts of light pierced through the foliage and fell around us like blades. Somewhere we could hear water tumbling down with a crystalline sound as if it were flowing along a bed of clean, well-polished pebbles. Its clear bubbling enveloped this place and perhaps that is why these tall, heavy trees, these exposed roots, like supernatural growths, and these ferns sprouting out of the bark did not frighten us. David went up to a tree, felt a fern between his fingers, slowly ran his hand over the damp bark before finally leaning his whole body against the tree, as if he were hugging it in his arms. I had never seen anyone behave like this before, but I made not the slightest sound, the least movement for I was afraid of shattering something sacred. I looked at him, his arms around the trunk, his legs pale and trembling, emerging like two pallid tubes from his blue shorts, his white skin against the fern. When he had finished he picked up the stick he had leaned against the tree and came slowly towards me, limping. I would have given anything for him to have left that stick and come running, as he used to, lopsidedly, and for his blond hair to have bounced up and down on his head. He smiled at me, turning up one corner of his mouth first, his head a little on one side, which filled me with boundless sadness, I do not know why, and I looked away so that he would not see the tears on my cheeks.

We were exhausted. I ached all over and had a taste of plaster in my mouth. We sat down in the hollow of a tree. The roots made a V at the foot of the tree and they were so thick and high that one could lean against them. David put his head on my shoulder, as he used to in the evening at the prison. My legs were heavy and my head was throbbing from an increasingly intense pain, I remember, but I can recall the silence and the feeling of incredible peace that this brought us. I stroked his blond hair repeatedly with the flat of my hand, for I knew this action was soothing. My mother did it for us at Mapou, Anil did it for me when I was ill and laid low with my cough.

I should have liked to say that David spoke to me,

I should have liked to say that he sang one more time, I should have liked to say that he hugged me tight in his arms one last time, I should have liked to say that I was aware of something, a sigh, a word, one breath longer than another, anything at all that might have made me understand that the moment had come, but no, I was aware of nothing. I stroked his hair for a long time, I had a shooting pain in my hand, but I did not stop until he had closed his eyes. Did he die there, beneath my hand, on my shoulder? Did I believe he was falling asleep, whereas in truth he was going?

When I woke up I found it hard to realize where I was. It was almost cool and I felt David's curls on my neck, his weight on my shoulder and somewhere the water was flowing. I disengaged my shoulder as delicately as possible, supporting David's head and laying it down upon a root. I tried to get up, but in vain. My back was as stiff as concrete, thousands of ants seemed to be climbing over my legs. I crawled for a moment before being able to stand up. I took several steps, but each time I placed a foot upon the ground I felt as if my bones were going to disintegrate, as if my legs could not bear my weight for long. I walked round the clearing as well as I could, step by step, hoping that my muscles would loosen up. My eyes were burning, I had only one desire, to lie down and sleep, and I told myself I had the fever too.

To tell *precisely*. I began by calling to him. Wake up, David, I said several times. I went up to him, I spoke his name close to his ear, I shook him very gently, but his body slipped and was stretched out full length. That was when I saw his chain with the Star of David on the ground. I picked it up and put it in my pocket so that it would not get forgotten there. That was a sign, sure enough, there I had been, searching for them in the sky, in the clouds, in the flight of birds, yet I paid no attention to this golden chain that had come undone and I would never have thought I should be keeping that Star of David for sixty years. I called to him and shook him a little more energetically, but to no avail. Like an engine starting up, roaring louder and louder, I felt my fear mounting. I found it hard to stay upright, but fear made me forget my pain. I sprinkled water on his face, drops of it at first, but as that had no effect I emptied the whole bottle over his head. I snatched up a fern frond and tried to wake him by tickling his ears. But he did not stir. My ears were buzzing, I began shouting. David! Wake up! I lifted one of his eyelids and I remember his green pupil which was right up high, as if he were trying to look above his head. I brought my face close to this pupil, hoping he might see me and wake up. But he remained unmoving.

Then, so as to have something to occupy my hands, my mind, so as not to see, so as not to understand, I did everything I could to wake him and it grieves me greatly to say this today. I tried to make him stand up, to swing him across my shoulder, I shouted at him, I yelled his name in his ear, I shook him, I threatened to leave him there if he did not wake up, I put my arms under his armpits, I lifted him, I dragged his body along for several yards and I ended up like that, with his body motionless, his head lolling forward, his arms dangling and I no longer dared move. But soon my painful legs began to shake and I could only think of one thing, not to let go of him, not to let go of him and my accursed legs were howling, there was this hellish pain boring into me everywhere, but I did not let go of him, I held on to him tightly, and even when my body refused to listen to me any more and I caved in myself, I held him pressed against me. God knows how I failed to respect David at that moment, I should have left him in peace, but I had promised not to abandon him.

On the ground, I clung to him and I wept and pleaded, as I have never had the chance to do with those others whom I have lost. There is no need to dwell on what I said. Irrespective of country, language, age, social status, what we say at such times is no more than a variation on the same phrases, the same words. *Don't leave me.* I ached everywhere, there was a taste of blood in my mouth, but I went on pleading, I was begging him to wake up. After a moment I laid his head on my shoulder and stroked his hair with the flat of my hand. I knew this action made one feel better. My heart was bursting with grief, it is as simple as that and amid the sultry heat of the trees and ferns I wept, I wept like the child I was.

I believe I should never have moved, I should have ended up dying in that dark and silent spot, too, if they had not come searching for us.

When I heard the first sounds of barking in the distance, despite my leaden body, I did not hesitate for a second. The physical strength of a creature at bay is incredible. I turned in such a way that my back fitted against David's chest. I grasped both his arms, I crossed them around my neck and with one hard movement I raised myself onto my knees. I could hear the dogs coming closer, but I was not afraid. I thought about that bundle of linen and tried to spread David's weight across my back, more towards my shoulders than the small of my back. I bent a little more and stood up, gritting my teeth. Keeping his arms firmly round my neck, I staggered and tried to run. I could not manage this but I moved forward, step by step. David slipped this way and that, I thought about the bundle and I thought about my mother and her joy at seeing us again, the two of us. She would know what medicines David needed, yes, she would know what to do, who to appeal to, who to plead with, who to pray to. Yes, I was on my way once more, towards the house deep in the forest and my mother would go out and find her plants, her roots, her leaves. Mapou no longer mattered, I had not thought once about Anil, my whole being was engaged on taking David home. I was bent double, David's feet were trailing on the ground behind me but I did not stop walking. I was following a mossy, shady path and everywhere, in front of me, under my feet, glimpsed out of the corners of my eyes, there were these soft, velvety ferns. I was telling David we would not be separated, I was making this promise to him once more. As I had in the forest, the first time he had followed me, I spoke each word distinctly, articulating as if I were in school. I was not afraid, I was in appalling pain, but I had the blazing courage of timorous and unhappy children.

When they appeared in front of us, the giants, the policemen in their blue, black and white uniforms, with their gleaming truncheons and the dogs leaping towards us as if we were rObbers, rUnaways and bAd mEn, when they saw me, with David on my back, is it true that I shouted and howled like a wild beast, as my mother has often told me? Is it true that it took two of them to wrest David from my grasp? Or did I stagger and shed all the tears in my body, as I do now, sixty years later, over his grave?

15

WHEN THE POLICEMEN FOUND US IN THE forest, David and me, we were only an hour's walk away from the prison. Three days, three days of wandering round and round Beau-Bassin, that was all we had done. David was dead and I, for my part, had poliomyelitis. They did not take his body back to the prison, they buried him here at Saint-Martin, in the Jewish cemetery. Beau-Bassin prison was in quarantine as the polio epidemic was rife throughout the island. The policemen wanted to take me to the hospital in the north, but my mother pleaded with them and they settled for handing me back. My mother is the one who told me all this. My memory had come to a stop in that cool, wooded glade, while

I was carrying David's body amid the ferns and shade and howling.

For two months my mother massaged me with herbs, oils and I don't know what besides. She made me drink decoctions and infusions. Once the sun rose she would be busy creating her mixtures of oils and herbs in her tin-plated copper bowl, and one of my earliest memories of the time after David is the regular click of the spoon against this vessel. In May 1945 three medical orderlies in blue tunics came looking for me. They were travelling from village to village, taking away children who had survived polio so as to fit an orthopaedic apparatus to their feet. My mother hid me in the shed where we had hidden David and pretended not to understand. They came back the following day and then, after that, they gave up, why put pressure on a poor family?

For a whole year, I stayed at home, lying down for a great part of the day, sometimes weeping for hours at a time. My father no longer addressed a word to me. This is something few people can believe and yet up to his death in 1960 he never spoke to me again. When he had something to communicate to me he went via my mother. The prison governor had dismissed him after they had found David with me and from now on he worked as a tinsmith's assistant at a workshop in the town. When he came home he brought with him a metallic smell that made one grind one's teeth. Sometimes he raised his hand against my mother and from my bed I would yell, as I would never have believed myself capable of doing, and go on until he came charging into the room, ready to shove my cry down my throat. But he never struck me again, never. From now on all I had to protect my mother was this performance. He would stop when he saw me, I do not know why I had this effect on him after my flight. He would spit out two or three oaths, slap his palms together and walk out. It was an appalling year for me, and I am not ashamed to say that every morning I prayed that I would die. I was ten.

Nothing happened to me, however, on the contrary I was cured of poliomyelitis, I do not wear a caliper, despite my atrophied left calf and a slight limp. In my youth I was able to run very fast. I remember that in the '60s a magazine published an article on the 1945 polio epidemic and they interviewed me. In the article the journalist spoke of my case as a "miracle cure" and I doubt if he knew quite how right he was.

Nowadays I sometimes encounter people of my age who have this apparatus with a built-up heel on their feet, black and monstrous, and I look at them with sympathy and a faint feeling of guilt. I do not dare to tell them that I, too, had polio but was lucky enough to have a mother who loved me more than anything else in the world and who was something of a sorceress. My mother could neither read nor write and when it was necessary to sign papers she would press her thumb into an ink-pad without shame. Every time I feel I know all the answers, I think about that, her blue thumb-print, and this puts me in my place. Towards the end of her life this mother who could neither read nor write wanted to go and live in a retirement home at Albion on the north-west coast. It was a white, sunlit place, dazzlingly hot, and you had to screw up your eyes to look at the sea. I did not like the idea of my mother living there, exactly why it is hard to say, perhaps because she had insisted so firmly on going there, perhaps because she was depriving me of the only duty left to me, now that my son was grown up and I was a widower: that of looking after her, as she had looked after me.

To be honest, it was an extremely pleasant establishment. Set amid casuarina trees and tall banyans, a red roof that could be seen from a long way off, a great satellite dish for viewing a hundred television channels, flowers everywhere, a tranquillity in which one could almost hear the sun's rays heating up the walls, it was just like a hotel. My mother had a little apartment there, and what a far cry it was from Mapou and Beau-Bassin! I believe she enjoyed this change greatly, this new life with women friends to chat to about nothing, a weekly picnic organized at the other end of the island, games of cards in the afternoon, yoga classes for the brave and TV in the evenings before falling asleep with the window open. Every time I visited her I would kiss her as I was leaving, look her straight in the eye and ask her if she would like to return home, telling myself that if I saw the slightest doubt reflected in her eyes, the least shadow, I should pack her suitcase on the spot. But no, she would slip her arm through mine, burst out laughing and push me towards the door. Unfailingly, in the courtyard, I would look back towards her apartment and she would be there on her balcony, with her little smile, one hand shading her eyes, the other waving to me, and I felt a fiercely painful lump in my throat. I pictured her back in our house in the forest, her shoulders hunched, as if forever prepared to receive blows, I pictured her with her mixtures, her potions and her magic formulas. I pictured her falling over, battered by my father, and I felt the sudden weight of her in my hands. I pictured her with the red parakeet and I heard her burst of laughter at David. I thought about those long months when every morning and every evening she massaged my legs to heal me. And there, this little scrap of a woman, smiling on the balcony, in full, bright sunlight, this was her and at the same time it was not her, and, on the return journey I always ended up in tears over it, this illusory happiness at the end, over all the things that had come much too late to erase everything else.

During her last years did she think about death the way I think about it today? The great whirlwind that has done its work around me, slowly nibbling away bit by bit. Anil, Vinod, David, my father, my wife, my mother.

One day I asked her if she knew who the people were in the prison at Beau-Bassin. She said the word used to be that they were immigrants from Europe and their ship had run aground on the island on the way to Australia.

"He didn't tell you anything else?"

This pronoun, "he" arrived fairly late between my mother and me. Earlier I think I used to say "*mon père*," but I never said "*papa*".

"No. He never talked to me about his work."

"Did you know there was a war in Europe at that time?"

"Yes, I knew. There were men at Mapou who enlisted in the army. You could earn a better living with a gun than a billhook, you know. They got clothes, they got food, and they sent money to their families."

"So you knew about the war? Why did you never talk to me about it?"

"I don't know. I never thought about it."

I had spoken my last sentence rather fiercely, but afterwards I regretted this, for clearly she had had other things to think about, her two dead sons, her violent husband, her younger son, silent and wild.

When Beau-Bassin prison was empty, when I finally went back to school I never talked about David to anyone at all. I never asked questions, I never told what had happened to me, I never cried out in pain, I picked myself up and went on. When my mother asked me where I had meant to go with David, I had replied: to join Anil at Mapou. She had gently responded with words people say to children, Anil is in heaven, and she had made me promise never to go off like that again. And I never had the urge to find Anil any more, for, strange as it may seem, now that David was gone, I felt that Anil was well and truly dead, too.

On my way to school, walking along in the cool of the morning with the dew glistening on the grass, gleaming in the silence, within me there was a buzzing vacuum. I had begun slipping into holes again, burying my face in the earth, camouflaging myself in bushes and climbing into the branches of trees to hide. I would go close to the prison and spend hours watching that empty, dirty, abandoned compound. It was only there, at that spot where I had seen David for the first time, only there that I allowed myself to cry. Just like the Beau-Bassin prison from now on, my life was empty, too, and I started talking when I was alone, I was talking to my brothers. I was telling David about things. When I closed my eyes, Anil, Vinod, David and I formed an indivisible brotherhood and sometimes, in my dreams, I had a few blond strands of hair.

Time passed. While the forest grew lush again each winter and the fruits swelled with juice each summer, I was growing. Sometimes I took out David's chain from the hiding-place in the wardrobe. I kept it around my finger like a rosary, I closed my eyes and the certainty of my friendship with David came back to me.

In 1950 I was fourteen and I had obtained that famous scholarship Mademoiselle Elsa had spoken about to my mother. For a year now I had become a head taller than my father, and in the mornings I felt a kind of suppressed anger and would never say a word to my mother. She bustled around me, poor woman, preparing my tea, my bread, she was proud of me, she was no longer so afraid, she watched me go and I did not so much as glance at her. As I went along I would pick up a stone and throw it a long way, in front of me or into the forest, then take another and a third and a fourth and go on throwing them, the anger rising into my eyes, giving a kind of shout at each throw, halfway between a sob and a grunt of effort, until there were no more stones. If I happened to pick up a stick of whatever kind, a reflex action we all have when out walking, I would suddenly remember and smash the stick against a tree, against the ground, demolish it, shatter it until only splinters and marks were left in my hands. At school I was forever shrugging my shoulders, I did not speak, I had an alarming way of clenching my jaw and holding my breath until the veins on my neck and forehead stood out. Sometimes my fists itched and I smashed them against a table, a wall, a tree-trunk and, once or twice, against a face. I was tamping down my sadness and my memories with this rage. When, on rare occasions, I thought about what I was doing, what I was turning into – the way I had of no longer looking at my mother, of walking with long strides, of turning my head swiftly, making abrupt gestures, flaring up, clenching my fists, not speaking, striking out blindly – I knew whom I resembled. And this idea, this obvious fact, that in the end I was simply my father's son, gave me suicidal impulses, and it grieved me once more that, out of all those good and just men who had been dormant in Anil, Vinod and David, I was the one who had survived. I am convinced I might have done something stupid, I cannot tell what, really beaten somebody up, had a fight with my father, thrown myself into the sea, who knows? I should certainly have left the straight and narrow, as they say.

But we had this history class. I was fourteen and for a whole week, from 10 a.m. to noon, the teacher, a somewhat pedantic man, whose name was that of a flower but I cannot now recall which, told us about the Second World War. This was 1950 and, incredible as it may seem today, it was the first time I had ever heard it spoken about. He unrolled a great map, with curved arrows, to show the advances, the invasions, the landings. Then he spoke about the Jews. How can I convey what was awakened in me when this teacher spoke of pogroms, yellow stars, extermination, death camps, gas chambers? I was horrified by what I learned, but at the same time happy for the first time in a long while: David had come back. I would get up in the morning and think about my friend. I remembered the way he did his long jump, his lopsided walk. This made me sad, but it made me smile, too, and I forgot about throwing stones, smashing sticks, jostling other pupils. I thought again about my nights in prison, the singing at the prison, my mother and the parakeet, and all these memories kept me company.

I was waiting for the teacher finally to talk about them, the ones who were at Beau-Bassin and who, my mother told me, had taken another ship. And whether what the teacher talked about had taken place anywhere here? Those horrible things, chimneys like the one at Mapou, but where, instead of sugar canes crackling in the fire, there were men, women and children. I was squirming so much I could no longer stay on my chair. On the Friday when the teacher announced that the following week he would be talking about Napoleon Bonaparte I put up my hand. It should be said that in those days pupils rarely spoke unless they were spoken to.

"Yes, Raj?"

"Sir, could you tell us about the Jews who came here?"

"I beg your pardon?"

"Could you tell us, please, about the Jews who came here?"

"But there were no Jews here. What put that idea into your head? Do you think they swam here? All the way from Europe. Really?"

I do not know who started laughing first and, after all, it makes no odds. I sat down while the rest of the class and even the teacher were doubled up with mirth. The fact that for a long time the others made fun of me, that the following week the teacher asked me, to the great delight of the whole class, if I thought Napoleon had come to our island as well, all of this made no odds. What matters was that my rage had disappeared, that finally the little Raj I had been was not completely dead and you can say what you like, believe what you like, no-one will ever take away from me the profound conviction that David had in some way returned to set me on the right road and that, throughout my life, he has been my good angel.

I had to wait until 1973 to learn how the Jews of Beau-Bassin had come to the island.

I was a happy man at the time in 1973. After leaving school I had completed a three-year training to be a teacher. Little Raj was quietly dormant in my heart, I had bought a red box to keep David's chain in, and my wife – the only person to whom I had told this story – kept it with the jewellery she had been given at the time of our marriage. In 1973 I was young and strong, the years at Mapou and Beau-Bassin had finally made of me, I hope, a just, honest and industrious man. I looked after my son, my wife and my mother, I had a little house surrounded by flowers and fruit trees and when I came home in the evening, having spent the whole day teaching children to read and write, my family would be waiting for me, happy to see me. How good that time was when I had the feeling that I was being useful and that my love sustained my house, my wife, my son, my strong and young mother. At that moment, happy, as I was, when I finally learned David's true story, I cracked like a dry, rotten branch.

We lived in a small village on the eastern side of the country. I was surrounded by those of my nearest and dearest who were still alive and felt as if the years of sorrow were behind me. My father had died in 1960 and I remember how, as I lit his funeral pyre, the tears rolled down my cheeks and I wondered how I could weep for someone who had beaten me and made me suffer so much.

It was a Sunday and I was very fond of Sundays at that time. In the morning we would eat breakfast together and we had cheese and jam. My wife would grate the cheese and it felt to me as if my son and I were of the same age, each watching the little mound of pale yellow, our eyes round with desire. My mother would consume it one shaving at a time, and it still makes me smile today as I picture her ceremoniously slipping each tiny scrap of cheese into her mouth. Then, while my wife and my mother were preparing a copious lunch, I would take my son to the centre of the village, a mile and a half away, to buy the newspaper. That was quite something, too. I would hold his hand on the way and our neighbours would greet me respectfully, for I was a schoolteacher. We would cross a field of sugar cane and take a road bordered with flame trees, passing other houses to reach the centre of the village. Here, there was an ironmonger's, a bicycle-repair shop and a grocer's, which sold a little of everything: tobacco, alcohol, vegetables, jam, sweets and the newspaper. The proprietor only ordered ten copies and he kept them prominently in a display case, as if they were luxury items. My son and I would take some time to get there because we often stopped to talk to other villagers and, as with a doctor, everyone had something to say to me. At the end of each of our conversations on the way to the grocer's they would remark: "You're going to buy your paper, aren't you?" And on the way back they would say: "So you've got your paper now!"

My son would choose a sweet, some chewing-gum, a fizzy drink, and he took some time to make his choice, and as it was Sunday I left him to it, I chatted with the men at the counter and it was very pleasant. On the way back I picked wild flowers for my wife and I am pretty sure that in our villages in those days I was the only man to do that. When we got home the meal was almost ready, blushing, my wife put the flowers into a glass – was she thinking about our first rendezvous at the harbour perhaps? – and we had lunch. Afterwards I would read the newspaper sitting on the wicker reclining chair under the big mango tree. There was a special atmosphere in the air and I was happy to be alive. It was there, beneath a mango tree, that I learned how all those Jews had truly come to the island. It was a short article on page 6 and it gave an account of a small ceremony at the Saint-Martin cemetery.

> On Friday morning the Jewish cemetery at Saint-Martin was the scene of unusual animation. A delegation of ten people, on a visit from the United States, gathered beside the graves of the 127 Jews who died in exile on Mauritius during the Second World War. Among the delegation were four former exiles who, twenty-eight years after leaving the country, have just returned to set foot upon this soil which they hated for so long.
>
> It is an item of world history which remains little known to this day. For, despite its remoteness from Europe, the Island of Mauritius did play a role at the time of the Second World War. On 26 December 1940 the *Atlantic* landed at Port-Louis with some 1,500 Jews on board. Among them were Austrians, Poles and Czechs, in flight from Nazism following the autumn of 1939. Some of them had boarded the ship at Bratislava, others at Tulcea in Romania. All wanted to go to Palestine, then subject to a British mandate. Unfortunately, on their arrival at the port of

Haifa and lacking immigration documents in good order, they were quite simply considered by the British Foreign Office and the British Colonial Office to be illegal immigrants. The *Atlantic* was turned away and the Jews were deported to the Island of Mauritius, then a British colony. The Jews were interned at Beau-Bassin prison until August 1945 and during the course of these four years of exile 127 of them died and were buried at Saint-Martin.

During the course of a poignant ceremony in which a small bunch of flowers was placed on each grave, a former exile, Hannah, born in Prague in 1925, made a declaration to us in the presence of the delegation and some bystanders: "We were locked up at Beau-Bassin for four years and we didn't understand why we were in prison in a country so far away from everything. No-one knew of our existence, we were pariahs, our daily life was painful and we didn't have the right to leave. Every day we dreamed of only one thing: travelling to Eretz. When we finally left in August 1945, I swore, like many of those prisoners, never to set foot on Mauritius again. But I am here today and my thoughts are with my friends from the *Atlantic* and with all those Jews who didn't have the good fortune like me to survive.

> The delegation was then received by the Minister of Foreign Affairs who gave assurances to its members about the proper maintenance of the cemetery and the impending creation of a memorial committee for the Jews imprisoned on Mauritius. Unfortunately not all the details of this dramatic episode in our history will be known since the archives of the British Foreign Office remain classified.

The blood was pounding ever more fiercely in my temples as I read the article. I remember burying my head in my hands and weeping, as I had not wept for years. And when I tried to get up from my chair to wash my face I collapsed like a tree-trunk blown over in a cyclone, my heart not strong enough to withstand this electric shock of memories.

From that time forth I have never ceased searching for David in books, in films and archives, to try to catch a momentary glimpse of how he had lived during those terrible years. A voice, words, an emotion that might have been his, that of a child aged five, boarding a ship with his parents which was crammed with refugees, bound for Palestine. When and how did his parents die? Who took him in their arms to comfort him at that moment? Who watched over him? I do not know.

As I press home the red box containing his star between the black granite of his gravestone and the earth, I picture that blond child again, his magnificent long-jumping, his good-natured face silhouetted against the sky and the foliage of the trees, the red parakeet perched on his golden hair and I tell myself that in a minute I shall recount David's story to my son, so that he, too, may remember.

FINIS